THE

JERICHO

JOURNALS

THE JERICHO
JOURNALS

by

John Scherber

The Sixteenth Book in the Murder in Mexico Series

San Miguel Allende Books
San Miguel de Allende, Gto., Mexico

ACKNOWLEDGMENTS

Any book starts as an idea, and by its completion becomes a joint effort.

Thanks to all the following:

Lander Rodriguez for the cover design.
Julio Mendez for website design.

Special thanks to Georges Mazilu for allowing me to use his painting, *Madonna in a Venetian Costume* on the cover and within the pages of this book. The paintings of Georges Mazilu are represented by Turner Carroll Gallery, Santa Fe, New Mexico.

To my writer's work group in San Miguel for constant input and critiques: Florence Grende, Christina Johnson, Michael Landfair, Marcia Loy, and Lynda Schor.

For editing and many valuable suggestions: my wife, Kristine Scherber.

ISBN: 978-0-9906551-4-5

San Miguel Allende Books
San Miguel de Allende, GTO, México.
www.sanmiguelallendebooks.com

Also by John Scherber

FICTION

What people greatly desire to believe is quite as interesting as the truth, and generally it is more immediately influential.

   -Robertson Davies, *The Merry Heart*

Only art can save us from the truth.

   -Derek Hamilton, *A Philosophy for Our Time.*

For Kristine

CHAPTER ONE

One day, about fourteen months ago, the painter Edward Jericho disappeared. While he was fairly well known locally, he was not famous beyond our borders, and not many people were aware of his absence at first. I rarely ran into him more than three or four times a year, so his departure wasn't obvious to me.

People from the United States and Canada come and go here in San Miguel de Allende with no special regularity, since this is a destination town in the way Aspen or San Francisco is, or Cape Cod in the summer. Set in the mountains of central México, it is at once an art colony, an active music scene, a retirement haven where the dollar can be stretched to new limits, and a refuge for writers both famous and anonymous. Besides the tourists, for longer sojourns it draws people with a slightly different take on living. A comfortable niche awaits those who are chasing an unconventional dream, a walk on the wild side later in life with sensible shoes, or an expatriate lifestyle free of hometown or family expectations.

That description fit Edward Jericho perfectly. He was known to stand out as an eccentric in a town replete with eccentrics. Since this absence had gone on longer than any others, when speculation began to spread about his whereabouts I still heard little conjecture that he might have come to harm. The subtext was more that he was perfectly capable of wandering off for his own obscure and private reasons, even for fourteen months. At times it sounded as if people were starting to reassure themselves out loud.

Charming and historic, at its center a nearly literal snapshot of colonial México but for the cars and more interesting paint colors, the town of San Miguel is still not for everyone. Some restless exiles eventually hoist their anchor and sail off to the next beckoning Shangri-La. Rumors about these comings and goings are rampant among the expat community of eight thousand, seeming to dance lightly from tongue to tongue. About a month ago I heard some gossip that an auction was going to be held to sell off the household and studio effects Jericho had left behind. This suddenly gave his extended absence a sharper and unwelcome edge.

Although he was rumored to have some family money, always a boon to any artist, he was renting the fine old house he lived in, a transient condition suited to a vagabond lifestyle.

The story went that he had simply abandoned

what appeared to be all his worldly possessions, right down to his shoes and clothing. Later, a woman who had been working in the house to organize his belongings for the auction noticed that a half finished painting was still resting on his easel when she arrived to prepare the catalogue. Next to it, the brushes standing upright in a small ceramic vase had never been cleaned, and their bristles were now hardened into solid colors. Dried paint inched its way across his palette in serpentine squiggles. As a painter myself, I began to suspect that something had to be uncomfortably suspicious about Edward Jericho's protracted absence. Even if we like to think of ourselves as footloose and free to roam on impulse, wouldn't we at least clean our brushes and take along our shoes?

High quality brushes are expensive anywhere, and since Edward often demanded sable for his work, the types he needed were not always easy to locate in San Miguel. Serious painters can never settle for inferior ones, since they make up a vital part of a skilled technique. Next I heard that the landlord had been forced to go to court and finally received permission to auction off Edward's belongings to pay the back rent. That's not so easy to do here; squatters have more rights than they have in the States.

While Edward was successful in finding buyers for his work, for his subjects he preferred images from the past, and reproduced exquisite versions of

Renaissance or later mythological or devotional subjects originally painted by other artists. He was highly knowledgeable about the Pre-Raphaelites, a group of nineteenth century English painters who sought to return to the techniques and values of Italian painting before Raphael came on the scene around 1500.

Privately, I would have described Edward not as an artist, since he put none of his own ideas into these paintings, but as a serious and even profound student of art. Even if some people questioned his creativity, the sophistication of his technique was remarkable. He could paint masterfully in a wide variety of styles.

Still, he lacked both the passion and the originality it takes to develop important finished work from his own ideas and to create unique images. My partner, Maya Sanchez, whose command of nuanced English, particularly of the slang, is remarkable for a Mexican woman, even one as well educated as she is, once described Edward Jericho to me as *effete*.

Of course, as a visual artist, language is not my long suit, even English, and I had to look up that word. Decadent, or lacking in vigor, is the definition I found. Maya doesn't mind it when I sometimes tell her that her English is better than mine, although she never says that to me about my Spanish.

We both slightly knew his former live-in girlfriend, the poet Rocio Valdez. While she was not overtly sexy at first glance, never working at it, and was normally a person of restrained presentation, she was clearly sensual in subtle ways. I had noticed this even in the movement of her fingers. I didn't think she could ever take a less than passionate man as her companion for four years, which is how long she and Edward were together. My impression of her was that she was a woman who welcomed being loved, not to make her whole, to supply a missing part, but to add a subtle gloss to her own list of individual accomplishments.

Edward exhibited his work as the foremost talent in a collective gallery downtown on Mesones with four or five other artists. It was called Galeria Reflejo, and none of their work was at all similar. I knew him mainly because we traveled in the same crowd, although on different edges of it. He had once paid me the firm compliment of buying a *tondo* of mine (a circular painting, this one about thirteen inches in diameter) that was a plausible copy of a Raphael cherub I admired. Edward wouldn't have settled for anything less than a picture that required careful study to see whether it was genuine. Perhaps the same was true of his own painting.

Yes, I do copy things now and then too, but mainly to see how other artists work, because there is no better way to understand that than by pursuing those same effects, even 500 years after they were pioneered by someone else. Still, copies comprise less than one percent of my work.

Edward was also a horseman, although I didn't know how serious, which was why Maya came out to the loggia one morning as I was enjoying a second cup of coffee at the edge of the garden, and with subtle but inescapable emphasis slapped a copy of our weekly bilingual paper, *Atención*, down on the table next to me. I took this to mean she'd found something compelling inside, and I slipped my arm around her waist. My hand found her left hip. At thirty, an age she doesn't mind acknowledging to the right people, she still maintained the slender athletic figure she'd had when we got together eight years before. Her dark hair still had the touch of wave and hint of henna it had then. It reached to about three or four inches below her shoulders.

"Look at this," she said. "The rumor of Edward Jericho's household sale is true."

The half-page display ad announced the auction of the painter's furniture, collections, and studio effects for the coming Saturday. In the list of offerings, she had highlighted in luminous yellow-green one line in particular. *Lot 86: A large box of equestrian books and CDs. No tack.*

"Paul, check this out. He must have some wonderful resource books, and several of those dressage CDs are very expensive. They're letting them go as one lot!"

Maya had gotten back into riding, her high school passion, about a year and a half before, with the purchase of a Lusitano mare named Martina.

Three lines further down I pointed to another. *Lot 89: Assorted art books*. Any art books Jericho owned would likely be uncommon and the finest quality. The man was a collector in many areas. We had been in his house only once, for a party three years before, but some of his collections interested me more than his own painting. I had a suspicion that he might have some good reference material on the Pre-Raphaelites. Those books could fill a gap in my own painting reference library.

I also had a third reason for going to the auction, one of the best. I was curious to see what my own *tondo* of the Raphael cherub would bring. I think Edward had paid me about $800 for it.

At the same time it occurred to me that, because of the ambiguity of Edward's extended absence, this auction might also be of interest to the Paul Zacher Agency, the private detective group that bears my name. At the moment we didn't have a case underway, not that we needed to have one all the time. Often I'd rather be painting.

CHAPTER TWO

On Saturday morning the Jericho residence front door opened on time at nine A.M. for bidders who wished to preview the lots. At eleven sharp the auction would begin. I had invited Cody Williams to go with us. He's our partner in the Agency, a big man with a thirty-year background in homicide investigations in Illinois. Even at sixty-three years old he can still handle most things coming at him with no shortness of breath or of eagerness. In our last case, one we filed as *Lost in Chiapas*, he put down a near riot single-handedly. We don't usually operate with that much force, but when we need it, there is no substitute for Cody.

Maya is the Paul Zacher Agency president now, even though my name would still be on the office door if we had one. We usually receive our new clients in the great room of our house on Quebrada. She's got a master's degree in history and a fine eye for Mexican cultural detail, having grown up in Mexico City in a prominent business class family. While most people regard her as an attractive, refined woman, she's also killed two people in our earlier cases, but she doesn't care to talk about it. We've lived together for seven of our eight years as a couple.

The site of Edward's auction stood near the upper end of Privada de Baeza, a dead end street that begins from Parque Juarez and travels up a gentle slope along the right hand boundary of the old Villa Santa Monica. There the houses tend to be substantial and well kept, offering some long views within a quiet, almost isolated atmosphere. Any painter would love to live and work there. In the neighborhood he had chosen, the rent on Edward's house would not have been a bargain.

Maya and I drove up the slope, turned around to point down the hill, and parked. As the narrow cobblestone lane fell gradually away towards the park, a long stone wall on the right faced a row of well-preserved older houses. I felt that *decay* was a word not permitted here. Edward's place was an elegant but understated single-story house fronted by a mellow brown-gray façade; a complex color to mix, as I'm sure he well knew. Well-seasoned carved limestone casings framed the wide, paneled mesquite door. It was flanked by a few small ficus trees gathered against the front on each side; gripped to it, as the French do with fruit trees in the way they call *espalier.* The branches were spread out in a manner that displays both their beauty and logical restraint. I thought Edward must've appreciated this.

As we got out of the van I was again wondering why he had decided to disappear from this inviting situation, or did he have some unwanted assistance? Painters don't usually make many enemies, unless they're also in the detective business, and in our fifteen prior cases I've acquired my share of them.

Still, none of them have ever forced me out of my house for more than a day of surveillance.

The fabric banner hanging on the outer wall of Edward Jericho's rented house on Privada de Baeza read **Estate Auctions Bustamante**, Querétaro. Featuring yellow cursive script on a silky blue background, with a yellow fringe on all four sides, it rippled slightly in the morning breeze. I wondered if calling it an estate auction might have cast a shadow over the event. Still, there was no firm reason to think Edward was dead, only off being Edward somewhere in a place he found more interesting than San Miguel at that extended moment. He and Rocio Valdez had split up about six months before he disappeared. Since then I had seen her around town on three or four occasion, never with another man, although I could imagine she might be holding a few suitors at arm's length. Rocio was clearly not a woman you could rush into anything. I would characterize her demeanor as unflappable serenity, even if I couldn't have said how serene she remained during her breakup with

Edward. Among the large numbers of beautiful ethnic-looking women in this town, she had a taller and more distinctly uptown appearance, and not every man would be capable of matching her stride. Certainly anyone who wanted to try might have to offer her something at her own level of sophistication.

At the same time, there was nothing haughty about her. If Edward was around forty-five, Rocio was now probably nearly forty, my age, and when I had last seen her, she did not appear to miss being twenty-five or thirty in any way that showed. Perhaps she had realized those were only transient phases in her growth as a woman, a person, and a writer, and now she had entered into the real substance of her life. As a working poet, Rocio had the kind of obscure but loyal following that inspiring poets often have, one that guaranteed her a consistent if not large sale on each of her books. It was enough to keep her in print. I suspect that for writers, as for painters, finding an audience of people who get what you're trying to do is the greatest reward. A poet like Rocio often has her own contingent of followers that does not need to be overly large to still be effective. Hearing her name, people often nodded knowingly.

When Rocio's name was sometimes mentioned in my presence, I also nodded as if I knew her better than I really did. I suspected that lovers might have quoted her poetry to each other in the early hours of a satisfying

21

morning before dawn. Having spoken to her briefly but in some depth several times, I had long felt her insights were solid and intriguing. I could not have said whether she made a living from her work, but as a painter myself, that is never the first question I ask people in the arts.

Cody had arrived at the Jericho house before Maya and I did; we'd noticed his white Ford as we parked. Moving through the vestibule we saw him paused looking out through the garden windows, his feet spread apart and his hands clasped behind his back. The house was planned around a great room that fronted the entire long eastern edge of the courtyard garden. He stood in the center arch of five pairs of open doors, with his massive frame silhouetted against the indirect morning light.

"Look at him. I know he's onto something already," Maya said. "I can tell by the way he's standing. Is this going to turn into a case now? Is that why you asked him? I wonder if he even has his gun with him."

I shook my head. "When I called him I was only thinking of those fourteen months of absence. That's a long time. What else is there for Cody to be focused on? Did he find a big stash of Edward's football trading cards? That would get him interested."

"No, not from Edward, I wouldn't think."

Although I still recalled the charm of this long, high-ceilinged space from the single party I'd attended there, it was now broken up into furniture groupings and imported tables holding smaller auction lots. The studio occupied the far right end of the room, and there the three easels, the rolls of canvas, and the art supplies were offered. A track near the ceiling and a pair of drapes provided a way to screen it from the rest of the great room.

Edward's painting style was precise and detailed, using fast-drying acrylic paints. Since I prefer oil, I had no interest in his paint tubes or his brushes. Doing old master reproductions, he preferred to work on a smooth, fine-grained linen canvas. I'd rather use the coarse Russian variety from Yarka, where the nubby insistent weave pattern shows through the paint. It interrupts the sense of illusion some painters cultivate, because to me, it's never an illusion. It's only paint that needs to be taken on its own merits.

We came up behind Cody to say hello. Maya seized his hand, separating one from the pair behind his back. "Something hinky going on out there?" she said. This was a word she had picked up from his Illinois police jargon. American slang is her hobby.

As he turned to her his face took on a crafty, but still serious look. "Maybe. You never know." He looked at me. "But you must think so."

"I only wanted your take on things here. If this house is a crime scene, you'd pick up on it before anyone else." He only shrugged without further comment, but I knew he'd gotten the message before we arrived.

I hadn't read much of the catalogue listing of the auction lots in *Atención* beyond the art books, preferring to trust my own judgment once we were present to do our scan. Edward's furniture wasn't of much interest to us, since we already had what we needed to fill the house, and none of his was remarkable. Maya did like his long dining table with eight chairs done in a native style fabric, but our set was better, in my view. She happily moved off in search of the box of equestrian material, and I started to search for the art books. But when I turned back for a moment to face the entry, there was Edward's window-less art wall, displaying his collector pieces. None of his own paintings were hung there. I assumed they were all down at Galeria Reflejo on Mesones, and by now, few would remain that hadn't sold.

His art collection contained a number of old devotional paintings in good or restored condition. They were all far beyond the normal run of painterly skills common in colonial México, or what was called New Spain until about 200 years ago. Most of them that you see here, and they are not rare, are well used and often roughly handled, with the marks of leaking church ceilings and processional mistreatment. Many have some rippling canvas, tears or punctures, and often bear water damage or peeling paint. Devout grubby hands touching the saint's face don't promote longevity in art. Toward one end of this group my eye settled on my own

Raphael *tondo* copy, which stood out because it was so much fresher than the rest. It was one of a pair I had done, and the other had sold to a collector in Guadala-jara a few years before.

When my eye moved along two pictures farther to the left, I saw a painting that nearly stopped my breath.

I've long been a fan of the work of Georges Mazilu, a Romanian painter who has lived and worked in France for the past thirty years. This was a portrait titled, *Madonna in a Venetian Costume*, a formal piece about sixteen by twenty-two inches in size. Because Mazilu blithely inhabits a world a few degrees out of plumb from that of the rest of us, I've always enjoyed following his work online. Its eccentricity may be the principal reason I love it. Like Edward, Mazilu works in acrylic on fine-grained linen, but in the highly polished painterly tech-nique of the northern Renaissance. If you didn't know his style it would be hard to place him, since he inhabits no school or movement beyond his own oblique vision.

The figure in the picture was a young woman depicted from the waist up with a pert mouth and a benign but lively stare. She was posed wearing a long-sleeved green dress overlaid with a red vest. The fabric of both appeared to be crushed velvet, a great material for painters who enjoy rendering the way its textures collect light and shadow. Like much of Mazilu's work it had an insouciant charm that was at the same time

25

not fully comfortable. I had looked at other pieces of his many times and I knew merely from the size that Edward must have paid around $10,000 U.S. for it. Most people would want to consider it for a while before they bought one.

Maya loved Mazilu's work too. It appealed to her lawless nature as a Mexican, where individuality trumps group behavior every time. I decided to bid on it, thinking that the cataloguer appeared to have done little research on what the lots might be worth in a market larger than ours. There were no estimates or reserves listed in the catalogue. Values would be based on who showed up to bid, and what kind of mood they were in. The publicity had been limited. If I could get the painting cheaply enough I could always offer to sell it back to Edward for what I paid for it when he reappeared. In the meantime I could enjoy having it on my wall. I thought it unlikely that anyone local would know who Georges Mazilu was. When I moved on, it must have been with a pensive look on my face.

At the far end the display finished with a group of eight small watercolors that featured birds in mythological contexts, almost like Tarot card designs. These were from a local painter whose work I had seen before.

Yet, as if someone else had felt the auction house was not to be totally trusted to maximize the bidding, Edward's holdings of ancient bronze coins were already gone. Someone standing next to me looking at the same empty space on the wall said a dealer who knew something about Roman Israel had made a generous offer and purchased them before they appeared in the catalog. I recalled seeing some display frames there at the earlier party. Those coins had all been dark and crudely struck bronzes, charmless except to a historian or a connoisseur. I recalled that a few had been labeled *widow's mite*. Apparently Edward had also owned some Roman glass that went to the same dealer, but I didn't remember it in detail.

I briefly went through some of Edward's art books. The lot filled a single Lorelay banana box sitting on a hassock near the studio end of the room. I was correct in guessing there would be several premium collections of Pre-Raphaelite works, then more of Renaissance painting and a few others. Another volume was on Lord Leighton, not a Pre-Raphaelite, but a polished academic painter of Victorian London. You could imagine him working in a suit and tie. Along with about fifteen others, at the bottom were two smaller volumes marked *A Painter's Life, Vol. I, and Vol. II.* Possibly some artist's biography, I thought.

I still get calls to paint reproductions now and then, and they do help pay the bills if it's a project that interests me because it presents a challenge. This reference material could fill the gap when I was looking for period paintings to copy. I always identify the original painter and sign my own name on the back when I do this.

Maya was two tables away burrowing through the equestrian box and lost to the world. She appeared to be so focused that people seemed to be avoiding her. I sidled over to face her. Several oversize books were stacked to one side. I recognized Pat Parelli's name on one. Clinton Anderson was on another. Beneath this was a boxed set of ten DVDs, with eight or ten CDs stacked next to it. The one on top was called *Keys to Winning*.

"This is it," she said. Her eyes did not leave the box. "This is like striking gold."

"But isn't it also kind of sad? What do you think happened to his horse over all this time?"

She paused to look at me with a downward curve to her lips. "Edward had a six-year-old Azteca stallion he boarded at Rancho Aria when I was there too. I heard they sold it seven or eight months ago because he stopped paying board. You know how gossipy the equestrian community is. I thought Diego was a good horse, and I know they didn't have any trouble finding a new home for him. He went to someone in Guadalajara."

We'd had a murder case last year at Rancho Aria that we'd filed as *Uneasy Rider*. They charged about $500 a month for board, shoeing, and routine vet care, and Maya had started out there after she bought Martina.

I could see why the ranch owners might get impatient if the cash flow stopped, because the expenses never did. Since Maya had signed it, I had seen their boarding agreement, and it gave them the right to sell a horse if board payments stopped for longer than a six-month period, $3,000 worth of arrears.

Still, thinking Edward had lost his horse through his own negligent disappearance gave me pause. From what I had observed in Maya's relationship with Martina, most horses and owners could not be parted so casually. That relationship held a real bond. The times I went out to the ranch with her I could clearly see that Martina was happy to see her.

"What do you think about this?" I leaned across the table and spoke quietly. "Wasn't all this stuff important to him? If you were planning to leave for an extended period wouldn't you at least finish the canvas you were working on? I certainly would. Wouldn't you have your bank pay your rent and make the board payments for your horse? Apparently he had the money to do that, and it's not uncommon here for people who have another home elsewhere. I know people think of Edward as impulsive, but really, this goes far…"

She only shook her head as Cody came over.

"Did you see anything you want?" Maya said.

"Yeah, I did. What I want is a day in this house by myself with no crowds or interruptions and I will tell you what happened to Edward Jericho."

The auction began on time at eleven, following a late surge in the crowd that must have been driven by curiosity, because the newcomers wouldn't have had enough time to scan many of the lots. Suddenly the room was packed. Maya and I were both feeling gloomier as we thought about what all this must really mean for Edward. You could hear that the man had taken off again, but when you thought about his abandoned horse and saw the half-finished painting and the clotted brushes it appeared to have a more sinister significance.

Auctions are not that different, but what made this one stand out was that Maya got her equestrian box for the peso equivalent of $82. I got the book lot for $38. Best of all, I came in with the winning bid on the Mazilu painting at about $2150. That was a lot of dollars, but it meant to me that while a few bidders may have suspected what it was worth, they weren't sure enough to bet the farm. Sometimes the artist's eye pays off.

I wasn't disappointed to see Rocio Valdez buy my *tondo* five lots later, although she got it at an unconscionable steal, $425. Grinning, she waved at us, holding her number loft as the hammer went down. Five minutes later the auction was over.

But how foolish we were to think that the dispersal of Edward's belongings was an end, rather than a beginning.

CHAPTER THREE

As he predicted, Cody hadn't bid on anything. Perhaps if Edward Jericho had possessed a load of football memorabilia Cody might have found something he had to have. O J Simpson's unrecovered Bruno Magli shoes from the murder case certainly would've caught Cody's eye for hitting a high mark simultaneously in both crime and sports collectibles.

Maya and I stood in line in the dining area to pay for our boxes. One of the staff was wrapping the Mazilu, and we had to pay for that too before they would let us near it. As the group chatted around us I watched Cody move off toward the kitchen door that led into the garage. He stood there for a long thoughtful moment studying a short ceramic bar of key hooks fastened to the wall. Then he considered the door lock from both inside and outside. After that he wandered off in the direction of the front door in the vestibule near the other end of the great room. Finally he came back over to us as we waited. His pace was casual, conveying no special intent, although he was one of the few people there who wasn't carrying something.

"His car sold in the first round, but it's still in the garage. That mean anything to you?"

"I saw that," I said. "It only means he didn't drive off in it and they must've charged the battery before the auction. They'd have to start it up to show that it still runs." Just the fact that the car was still there didn't look good, either. How many people flee their past lives in a taxi?

"Right, and there are two sets of keys for it by that kitchen exit."

"So what's wrong with that?" said Maya. She was never an easy sell, but this time I wondered if she felt she'd missed something.

"Well, there are two sets of house keys too. That door has a double-cylinder deadbolt, so you need a key to lock it from either side. If you leave and only pull it shut behind you, the door doesn't lock, it only latches. You'd need to take one set of keys away with you to lock it and to get back in. It's an old fashioned system, but this is an old house. That was the way they used to do things."

We both looked at him for a moment before he went on, neither of us sure where this train of thought went.

"The same thing is true of the front door, I just

checked it. Both sets of keys are still there too. I think they would've been Edward's and Rocio's."

"Couldn't there have been a third set?" Maya said.

"I suppose, but in both places there are only hooks for two, plus two more for the cars keys in the kitchen. Of course, the landlord has his own set, and possibly the cleaning and gardening people too. I was just thinking of the normal comings and goings of the people who lived here."

The three of us stood there for a while, none of us prepared to go the next step. Finally I did, not liking it.

"Then I guess what you're suggesting is that Edward Jericho never left this house, did he?" I said this quietly, and the murmur of the crowd prevented anyone else from hearing it.

With a slight bend to her knees, Maya gave us her *here we go again* look.

"Right," Cody said. "I can't imagine he would walk off and leave the house open with all his collections and his art. To me it looks like Edward Jericho is still here on the property, somewhere. He always has been."

"And for the last fourteen months," Maya said thoughtfully.

With an identical instinct, we all turned and looked out into the garden. It had been minimally cared for since his departure. The plants were mostly high desert varieties native to the area so they hadn't required a lot of water. The landlord must've done some minimal maintenance just to keep the property looking decent, knowing it might come to this as Edward's absence continued. After we finished paying for the lots we pocketed our receipts and walked outside to the courtyard through the French doors. None of us looked happy.

The garden design was spare, almost modern. The main feature was defined by a line of *organos* cactus against the wall on three sides, the single shaft variety that could reach about fifteen feet in height. They rarely grew any arms, and when they did, they didn't stretch out much. Small succulents on a gravelly bed provided the ground cover. The rest of the garden inside this rectangle was paved with rough limestone squares radiating from a central fountain, a sunburst effect in dry pavers. We were all looking for the same thing, and we didn't need thirty years of experience like Cody had put in on the Peoria homicide squad to spot it. It would not, however, have been obvious if you weren't already searching for it. We separated and walked off the borders of the garden.

At the back corner on the right, along a length of about seven or eight feet, four of the five *organos* were shorter than the rest, and the fifth was failing, as if they'd been cut off and stuck back in. This was commonly done; they don't need any special rooting treatment. In that area the pea gravel layer below the plantings was irregular and sparse, and there were few of the small succulents. The ground surface had clearly been disturbed. Altogether it was not a display you would notice much in a garden that had been minimally cared for at best, one that had other failing plants as well, unless you were looking for something that shouldn't have been there at all.

"Look at this," Cody said, pointing as he squatted on the pavers. His thick blunt fingers outlined the margins between a dozen of them that bordered the plantings. Traces of the pea gravel were there too, although not in other areas nearby. It appeared to have been scraped off the soil and then imperfectly raked back from the pavers into the plantings. But it had not been completely swept out of the grooves between the stones. The topsoil had been disturbed and then carelessly replaced, possibly by someone in a rush to leave after committing a murder.

"I suspect Diego Delgado is probably working today," I said as I stood up. Cody pulled out his cell. Licenciado Delgado was our main contact in the San Miguel Judicial Police, the group that investigates major crimes, like kidnappings and murders. We had worked with him on nearly all of our fifteen prior cases. Cody walked off a few paces once the connection was made.

"What do you think?" I said to Maya "This is your call." As president of the Paul Zacher Agency she decides what cases she wants us to take. This one, of course, would pay us nothing, since no one had hired us. Since she writes the checks to pay the bills at the end, charity cases are usually the kiss of death for her, but not always if she can see some greater social benefit in working for nothing. We are not opposed to being occasionally charitable with our time.

'I don't think we can let an artist's murder go unsolved," she said. "That would be a terrible precedent." With an unconvincing grin she slipped her arm through mine. "Poor Edward."

"Of course poor Edward, but wouldn't we be second guessing Delgado if we got into this?" I said.

"What kind of guess can he generate at all," Cody said, catching up with us, "when the body has probably been unprotected in the ground for fourteen months? He'll be lucky to even come up with a cause of death if there isn't an obvious bullet hole in the skull. Anyway, he's coming over with a crew. I sensed a bit of reluctance, but I pointed out that we've never led him astray in all of our previous cases."

"Did that do it?" Maya said.

"Not quite. I also had to remind him that Paul got him out of prison on our first case."

"I always knew we'd have to play that card some day. So if this idea is correct, just how much would be left of Edward now?" I asked quietly. "More or less. I don't need a lot of detail in your answer."

Cody shrugged. "Subject to ground moisture, temperature, and ambient bacteria, not much more than bones, but perhaps the desiccated remnants of a few fleshy masses."

He had correctly identified the phrase we didn't want to hear. "In other words, it would not be a good subject for still life painting." It's always good to have an expert on staff to advise us about what to expect from a body that's been in the ground that long.

Maya was right. Poor Edward.

CHAPTER FOUR

As the president of the Paul Zacher Agency, Maya was also able to delegate the observation of the exhuming of long dead friends' bodies, so she volunteered to drive back to our place on Quebrada with the two auction boxes and the Mazilu painting taped between heavy cardboard sheets on both sides. Cody and I waited silently for Delgado and his crew. By the time they arrived more than an hour later, the crowd was almost entirely gone and little remained in the house to recall Edward's tenancy or lifestyle but for a few pieces of furniture awaiting the movers. I suspected the same was true of his body. Maya hadn't returned. It was probably going to take a call to bring her back, one saying Edward's remains had been bagged and removed. She'd probably still find a reason not to come back, like she was starting dinner, something I usually did.

Erratic as his presence had been, Edward Jericho had established a real position as the archaic, almost the *archival*, painter in San Miguel, and I hated to see that influence gone. Maybe as a fellow artist I saw myself in his situation. I couldn't help feeling how sad it was as we sat around waiting for Delgado, yawning and look-ing at our watches. Edward's easels had sold and his last, small, unfinished painting was sitting on the floor leaning against the wall waiting for someone to walk past and put his foot through it. It was a landscape, far from the subjects Edward was best at, and it was little more than sketched in with some color suggestions spotted here and there throughout. I stared at it for a long moment, trying to think whose work he might be copying, but I came up with no names. His crusted palette and caked brush-es were sitting next to a steel drum on wheels marked BASURA (trash) Bustamante. The scene didn't quite make sense to me, but I had other things on my mind. At least someone had bought Edward's unused paints and clean brushes.

I couldn't help but imagine my own brushes being wastefully sold off to strangers where no one knew what they were best used for. Here was the old partly stiffened squirrel tail beater I used to soften edges and blend one color into another. Here was the fine pricy sable for portrait eyebrows and other superfine de-tail. I always took extra care in cleaning it. Here was the number ten hog bristle flat for roughing in back-grounds or skimming the surface on a coarse weave to lay down a netting of overlay color that left the under layers visible for accent or contrast. Sad indeed.

As Paco Mora, the medical examiner, and Esquivel, the forensics officer, filed in with two shovel bearers behind them, we exchanged our usual greetings with Diego Delgado. One of the crew ominously trailed a large opaque black zippered bag. Cody filled Delgado in as we all walked back into the garden.

Delgado was shaking his head, as he always did when he entered a crime scene. "So Señor Eduardo Hericho (as he pronounced it) has been missing during these fourteen months and no complaint was ever filed to us downtown? Evidently he was a most popular man indeed, and is missed by all his close friends, I would say. Please call me sooner on the next time."

"It isn't that. He was something of an eccentric." I told him about Edward's tendency to disappear for months at a time with no warning. While this was mostly hearsay on my part, it was also true that no one that knew him had raised a private alarm; at least so far as any of us had heard. Perhaps Rocio had been more concerned, but I hadn't ever had a conversation about it with her. Speculation only began with the auction announcement. I thought he deserved better than that. The man's spirit was missing, but the alarm was sounded only when his rent failed to show up for months on end.

"I see," said Delgado. "You are saying now he

was a man who would eat flour tortillas every day when he could have corn."

This definition of an eccentric probably meant more to him than it did to me, and Maya wasn't back yet to explain it in a way I could more easily grasp. Cody, who preferred flour tortillas, only shrugged. He was always more about facts than theory.

Delgado stopped at what we believed was the burial site, hands behind his back, his right index finger trembling slightly as if it was getting ready to soon point at something.

"OK, let us stop at this place for a little. I can see your idea now how it goes, why judging from the ground it is to dig here. I hope we will find enough left of Señor Hericho to tell us the story of his passing." At a subtle gesture from his head the diggers started in.

We'd had an experience on an earlier case, one we filed as *Angel Face*, with a long dead corpse, one that had been thirty-one years in the ground, but that woman's body had been normally buried in a state-of-the-art coffin, and because of that, first class embalming, and some peculiar environmental conditions, her body had not decayed when we saw it. Expecting a different outcome this time, Cody and I found ourselves drifting away as the shovels probed deeper. This was a reliable measure of how we regarded digging up dead bodies. Neither of us objected to respectably bare bones. I owned a cleaned and polished medical school skull myself, one that I sometimes painted in a still life. However, incomplete decomposition prior to that stage was a different issue for us. It offered neither artistic possibilities nor much comfort.

"I just hate to see this," I said. "He was someone I knew, a painter, even."

"I hate to see it too, and I never met him," Cody said.

Delgado paced back and forth along the edge of the pavers in one of his brown suits, possibly the most worn of the set, since he had arrived expecting this would be an exhumation. None of us thought the body would be six feet under, since the murderer would have sought only concealment and anonymity, not eternity. So when one shovel struck a soft but resistant element that proved to be a piece of clothing, Cody and I retreated further to a stone table at the far corner of the courtyard and sat out the rest of the process. There would always be the forensic photos if we felt we needed to see the condition of Edward's remains. I didn't think we would. There are some, but not all the steps in this process where you can trust the local police and their procedures. Autopsies were usually one part where we did; we didn't need to watch.

Word of his purpose had traveled quickly upon Delgado's arrival, and everyone else in the house was already gone by the time he and his crew started to lift out the mostly unconnected, but not unrelated, parts of the victim's remains. From the fragmentary way they came out, I could see there was no shroud to help lift them into view. Edward had been interred in what he was wearing at his death.

CHAPTER FIVE

Edward's former partner of four years, Rocio Valdez, now lived in apartment number three on the second level of a massive old casa in *centro*. Fronting on Calle San Francisco, its peeling mango-colored façade revealed nothing whatever about the lush, if by now bruised and faded, seventeenth century interior.

San Francisco is a hard-working blue-collar thoroughfare during most of the day, and Rocio's block houses several different banks in other old mansions. The foot traffic is lively. But once I was inside the massive mesquite doors, the noise fell away as if it belonged to an era as yet unborn. The only sound within was the intimate murmur of a large, ornately carved multi-level limestone fountain in the center of the courtyard. A pair of porpoises would've had enough room to relax and even mildly cavort in the lowest and deepest basin of the three. Glancing into it as I passed, I saw only lazy goldfish.

On all four sides of the courtyard a tall, arcaded

gallery with a second level above faced this tame water feature. Although the echoing space had been roofed against the weather within recent times, numerous sky-lights allowed the sun to pour into the quadrangle as it had for the nearly four centuries before, when it was still open to the sky. In the far left corner I stopped and looked up toward Rocio's second floor. Was it a retreat from the active city for her? Anyone living in *centro* would want that kind of calm, but who knew about poets? I thought of them as even more obscure and untypical than painters, and still less likely to manage to earn a living. I climbed the hollowed marble steps to the second level and found the entrance to number three about half-way down the row. It was nearly five o'clock.

Two days had passed since Diego Delgado's forensic crew had exhumed the mostly decomposed body that could only belong to Edward Jericho. On the back rim of his gold-filled Raymond Weill watch the engraved initials had confirmed his identity. It was a $1600 Swiss handmade artifact that remained on his wrist, even if with a somewhat looser fit now. Why had the killer left it on his body? It clearly suggested to me that the motive in Edward's death had not been robbery, and to have that unusual watch in his possession would've condemned the killer if caught, and he may have considered that.

I had called Rocio Valdez to see if she would furnish me with more information about Edward's life and who might have wanted him dead. While she wasn't exactly eager to talk about her time with him, neither was she opposed to the idea in the circumstances. Her voice on the phone sounded as if she had seen something like this coming. I knew it would be an advantage that she already knew me, even if not well.

Rocio answered the door wearing a deep violet long-sleeved knit top with a cowl neck that suited her coloring perfectly, over a pair of black slacks. Too many Mexican women wear pink because they believe it's a feminine shade. It is that, but it often doesn't suit their skin tones as well as a deep violet. Rocio touched her dimpled cheek to mine briefly in greeting. Her hair was gathered by two mother-of-pearl combs behind her ears and suspended behind her head. With an oval face, her high cheekbones gave her a slightly Asian look. As they did whenever we met, her features tended to hold my eye.

"I'm terribly sorry about Edward's death," I said. "I've known for more than a year that he had gone some-where, but whoever thought it would end like this?"

"Please come in, Paul. I'm only glad to have some closure now, but I'm still reeling. I never could under-stand what happened to him." She led me into the room and closed the door. "He was upset when we separated, but that was six months before he disappeared. He had a lot of time to get over it. You and Maya were so smart to figure this out, I mean that he was still there."

"It was really our partner Cody who did. Had it ever happened when you were together that he just disappeared for a while?" I had already heard some of this, but I wanted to see if she could give me more detail.

Rocio nodded somberly. "When I first met Edward he had returned a week before from four months in Italy. Nobody knew where he'd been. Over time I learned you couldn't change him. He didn't care to be accountable to anyone. Whenever I was on the verge of calling the police about this last absence, even though I wasn't with him anymore, I thought about that time, and it stopped me. I know there were other times before that too, although when we were living together he always told me what he was planning and he was never gone as long as this. In fact, those three trips never lasted more than a month and a half."

She placed her cool hand on mine and led me into her parlor. For Rocio, as for many Mexican women, conversation with men she knew on the same social level was a contact sport. Her friendly touch meant no more than a way of connecting while she spoke.

Parlor is an old fashioned word for a room now, but that's exactly the way this huge house had been designed. It was densely and unashamedly old fashioned, even antique. It exuded the feeling of a gathering place for Spanish colonial aristocracy that had been long abandoned and was now divided among lesser folk who may have felt dwarfed under the tall ceilings that offered an elegance that few understood. A radical cutting-edge update from its original décor would've brought it up to about 1820, when México was a new country, just free of Spain. With the tall ceilings and massive stone window and door casings, that concept still worked quite well for today if you aren't a modernist, as I never have been. Standing there with Rocio I felt I had left the twenty-first century behind, as well as the twentieth and most of the nineteenth. That was not a problem.

The two large mullioned windows in this room, which had been designed for formally receiving guests, looked out through the arcaded portico and over the courtyard. The ancient walls were so thick that their louvered shutters easily folded up into recesses on both sides of the windows and disappeared to match the paneling. Throughout the room the walls were paneled with a vertical design, as if with a series of narrow doors. The effect was elegant. As part of this decor, I was pleased to see my copy of the Raphael *tondo* now hanging over the door to what had to be her bedroom. Edward had ordered a carved gilt frame for it.

In one corner a run of shoulder-high bookcases were filled to overflowing. The glass panel doors that fronted them lent an air of privacy to her collection. I had to resist the impulse to walk over and inspect her library.

Rocio Valdez was tall for a Mexican woman, about five-foot-eight, with a slender build, long graceful legs, and thick wavy hair that even gathered behind her head still reached below her shoulders. Her large eyes and her expressive and mobile mouth animated her face. When I turned to sit down next to her I was astounded to notice a full-length portrait of her on the wall next to the entrance where I'd come in. In that painting she was wearing a long dark green silk dress in a Victorian design. The luscious rendering of the draped fabric was as skillful and subtly shaded as that of her skin. The setting that filled the frame behind her was an entry she had just passed through. The grainy surfaces of that classical doorway were carved in buff-colored limestone. In this composition the intense colors of her hair and the dress played against the chiseled contours perfectly. A true masterpiece, I thought, even if it was not exactly like the original painting had been in all respects.

"I can see that this is Edward Jericho painting his rendition of Lord Frederic Leighton," I said. "And he captures that style extremely well. It's striking because I don't think I've ever seen a painting of Edward's before that's not a close copy of someone else."

"Well, that one is mostly a copy too, except for my head," she said. "It's lucky that Leighton's original model was also tall and had my proportions. A lot of those Victorian studio models were rather chunky by our standards. Edward could paint his own ideas if he wanted to, although he rarely seemed to. I'm happy to have this, especially now that he's gone. He gave it to me when we split up."

"The likeness is wonderful, and it's expressive in the same way you are in life. It's credible, if you know what I mean, like there is a real person behind the image. I can't believe he didn't want to do more of his own work, paint his own ideas. His skills were marvelous."

She shook her head with a small shrug. "I know, but still, I sometimes wonder what Edward meant by not giving me a likeness of himself or something personal of his, for example."

I could see that she genuinely meant this, so I didn't respond by saying that by painting her face so well into this picture, a very rare original touch from him, Edward had in fact done the very thing she most wanted. That she didn't perceive how far outside his comfort zone that was for him suggested other issues in their relationship. I couldn't imagine that he was ever easy to understand, even for someone as close as his lover. Now she was waiting for me to go on.

"Was it a difficult ending for you when you two parted?"

Rocio pursed her lips and made a random gesture with the fine fingers of her left hand. The light from the lamp at her shoulder caught three or four silver rings, all delicate in character.

"Aren't they all? But it wasn't nasty, if that's what you're asking. It wasn't really much of anything but over, but nonetheless still very sad because of that." She paused for a long moment and examined the portrait of herself again. I wanted to step up close to it and examine the detail, but she didn't rise to move any nearer so I didn't either.

"Will you have a cognac with me, Paul, before we get into this any further? I think I need to relax. I can feel the truth coming on in waves." The movement of her hands suggested she couldn't predict were that might go.

"Of course." I stood up as she did. "I hope you understand that I don't have any agenda in this conversation, Rocio, other than finding out what happened to Edward." My voice rose slightly in volume as she moved off into the kitchen.

"I'm glad of that." She turned to offer me a smile over her shoulder but did not respond any further. When she returned a moment later with a pair of elegant cut glass snifters I thought she was prepared to unwind a bit more. As she set them down, I once again noticed the easy grace of her movements, something that had always struck me about her. I've painted a fair number of elegant women, but I wasn't sure how I could portray on a still canvas that fluid sense of motion Rocio had. It made me think she might be better captured on film, and not necessarily with a soundtrack.

"Where are you from?" I said as we sat down again. "I don't recognize your accent in Spanish, slight as it is."

"I grew up in Monterrey."

"I've never been up there. I think I tend to avoid the northern states. Recently we spent some Zacher Agency time in Chiapas, though."

"The other end of the world, one of mists and mountains. A fit subject for poetry."

For us in the Agency it had been a voyage through hell and back. "Where did you learn English?"

"I went to school in California. College, but I already knew it then from attending a private high school here."

"As I said on the phone, I was hoping you could tell me more about Edward today. Although I'm sure Diego Delgado will do his best with his investigation, we've decided to take this on as a case, pro bono, you understand."

A much more somber cast came over her face as she studied her cognac for a moment. "Licenciado Delgado was here yesterday to show me a piece of fabric he kept in a zip lock bag. It was for identification, he said, so it had to stay sealed as evidence. That was no problem for me, since I really didn't want to touch it. I told him it came from the blue lab coat Edward always wore when he was painting. There was even a stain of crimson pigment on the hem. He also showed me Edward's watch."

"When I heard they'd found it I wondered why he would've worn an expensive watch like that when he was painting."

"Well, yes, he always did. It was protected, I suppose, by the lab coats he wore. The acrylic paints he used were water soluble until they dried." Rocio paused and, looking down at the ancient tiled floor, put the back of her right hand to her mouth. I said nothing for a while as she finally took a minute sip from her glass and set it on the table beside her. Although it was my turn to respond, I wasn't sure how to start.

"In the Agency," I said, finally, "we were shocked that Edward was still in the house, or on the property as you might say, all those fourteen months. I didn't know him well, but I had assumed he was off pursuing some object for his collections. Like one day he would simply reappear and as usual, say nothing about where he'd been all that time. He might've gone to Rangoon or Nairobi. I guess he was always rather private about what he was up to. Was that your sense of it too? You had a long time to observe him, more than most of us. And I don't know anyone who was as close to him as you were."

She shook her head slowly. "He was just that way,

and you're right. He would make no apologies or explanations, except what he said to me, which I never thought was very complete. He didn't think it had to be. If you were with him, then you had to accept him the way he was." Her voice dropped a note. "But maybe that's true of everyone. And I think he may have been on one of those quests when he died."

Hearing this I tried to decide whether she was referring to a specific goal rather than only the way he lived, but I didn't want to push her too hard.

"Tell me more about who Edward was to you. Who was he as a person, rather than as a painter?"

"Well, his only family is a brother in New Orleans, named Dillon Gericault."

I cocked my head. "Am I catching something different in the way you pronounced that last name?"

"Right. Edward and Dillon are descended from Theodore Gericault, the French painter who died of tuberculosis in the 1820s."

"Of course." I had the odd thought that Theodore could've comfortably died in the room where we sat, with a final delicate but nearly inaudible swoon. "A pioneer of the Romantic movement," I suggested.

"Yes, and the name was ironic because Romanticism was a painting style that Edward detested. He felt it was so dramatically overdone that early in his career he changed his name to Jericho. Most people couldn't tell the difference hearing it spoken, but he always enjoyed knowing the distinction. He also had a huge affection for the ancient civilizations, so he thought being called Jericho was a nice touch, a way to reframe that family name with some obscure implications he loved. I'm sure you looked through his collections before the auction."

Thinking of this prompted me to survey the furniture in that room for a moment. Her tastes were different from ours or anyone else's that I knew. The decor was French in style, with bleached wood, possibly beech, that bore traces of white paint in the recesses of the carvings, old rose-colored upholstery with touches of faded needlepoint, and eighteenth century legs and feet. All of it was well worn as if it had long been a witness to history. I had the idea that this apartment must have been rented furnished and this ensemble had been part of that room for many decades. Rocio was seated on a love seat and I sat on a delicate chair with arms. If he ever had a reason to come here, we would have to keep Cody off most of this furniture, with his six-foot-three height and 230 pounds of investigative skill.

"Do you know what became of Edward's personal effects? His clothing, his financial records and identification, his wallet and so on?"

She caught her breath. "I only know that the landlord, who is not a bad person, by the way, although I've heard he's taking a black eye from this now that it's become known what happened to Edward, packed all of that up and sent it off to Dillon a month or two before the auction. I never saw an inventory, because of course by that time I was long since out of Edward's life. Dillon handled it all from his end in New Orleans, and that was appropriate. Naturally, no one could have anticipated this."

"Exactly," I said.

"Still, I'm sure it would've been good if you'd had a chance to look through it."

"Of course, but no one knew he'd been murdered at that point."

"Well, someone did." She smiled sadly and took a tiny sip of her cognac. As she set her glass down it looked as if a pinpoint-size drop had stayed glistening on her lower lip.

"I assume Dillon is the heir?"

"Yes. I never was, I knew that well enough. To tell you the truth, with Edward I always felt just a bit… temporary. Is transitory a better word? I felt I was wonderfully interesting to him for a while, one in a long series of people and things that had their moment…" Her shoulders lifted in a small, refined shrug. "I think now that I stayed too long."

"In the sun of his gaze," I said softly. As it moved through the sky, I also thought, but did not say it.

Rocio's face didn't offer much elaboration

beyond that statement. To me, she looked like a person you'd struggle to hold onto once you had her in your life. The kind of woman that if I hadn't been so happily committed to Maya for the long haul I'd want to get to know better. She would not be anybody's idea of ordinary. It made me wonder whether Edward was a person who didn't form deep attachments. Perhaps he was always in search of the next big thing, and when he found it he would move on. I thought of it as serial focus. Maybe one of those big things had finally proven too big for him to handle. Success can be a trap that awaits some people. It can be tougher to handle than failure.

"Have you met Dillon?" I said.

"No, but I've talked to him on the phone several times about the plans for the memorial service here. He and Edward were twins. Not identical, but fraternal. I've seen photos of him and they looked similar, but not exactly alike."

"Did Edward have any enemies?" I said, smiling as if this were familiar terrain, since it was for me. "That's an old standard question, of course, but I can never skip it in this kind of conversation."

"I didn't know of any, but he didn't tell me everything. In his pursuits he might have made enemies easily. You probably think of painting as competing with yourself all the time, but for Edward, he came up against other people who often wanted the same thing he was searching for."

"Really? Were those things dangerous?"

"I'm not sure, but he certainly was secretive about them at times, although not always."

"Was he working on anything special when he disappeared?"

"In painting? I don't know. Aside from the auction, I was only at the house twice again after we split up. You saw what was on his easel when he…left. It was not another piece in the style of the northern Renaissance. It looked more like he was starting to sketch in a landscape, which I didn't understand. That was an odd subject for him, since he had no feeling for nature. I don't recall that he ever did one when I was with him, but he might've been trying to move on. I know I was." A curious look came over her face. "I still am, I suppose, after all this."

"How about something for his collections? Was there anything that you heard he was chasing? Perhaps a sale was happening somewhere far away that caught his attention?"

At this Rocio turned and stared into a corner of the room where an inlaid tall case clock stood isolated in a silence that suggested time had stopped long ago in these ancient chambers. The pendulum was at rest. As I followed her gaze and stared at it, from somewhere nearby in the building I could just make out a solo harpsichord piece beginning. I had thought we were alone. Rocio didn't react to it. She folded her hands on her lap.

"For several years Edward had been working on what I thought was a strange search, even for him, and it seemed from what he said toward the end that he was getting closer to it month by month. I never knew how seriously to take it myself, but his fixation on it was one of those things that helped finish our relationship. By the time the end came for us he had become obsessed by it. His painting was suffering and he hardly had a moment for me. Finally I just said to him one day, 'Call me if you ever find it. Then maybe we can have dinner and a conversation about something else for once.' I started packing that day, not seriously, but just to suggest what might be coming."

"You're saying he was obsessed more than he usually was with painting or his other collections?"

"There is no better word for it. You know this yourself, of course. People expect painters to be deeply absorbed in their work, but this went far beyond that."

"I do understand how that goes, but at some point you need a break, and you want to step back and refresh yourself with other things. The person you're with, what is she involved in? For Maya, it's horses, a rich and complex subject that is endlessly both demanding and engaging. Going out to dinner, talking about something completely unconnected to what you're painting is the best fix for this. Even taking a walk in the *jardín* or Parque Juarez."

Rocio nodded slowly. "For you and Maya I'm sure that worked, but Edward was more single-minded. He kept a handwritten diary that he hid behind the other books in his bookcase. He told me he was doing that, but I don't think he knew I was aware of where he kept it, and while I was curious about it, I never tried to look inside it. I suppose it went to Dillon with his other personal effects. You might contact him to see if he has it. I can give you his email address. Maybe he'll show it to you if he thinks it can help with solving Edward's death."

"Can you tell me what he was looking for that had him so engaged at the end?"

The volume of the harpsichord came up slightly, as if someone had opened a door or a pair of casement windows. If I hadn't been speaking with Rocio, I probably would've strained to listen more closely. It did not sound precisely like a Bach piece, but one with a feeling both lighter and busier, more like Scarlatti.

With her eyes now closed, Rocio Valdez had settled back into the loveseat, hands unmoving in her lap. Her long legs were crossed at the ankle and she appeared to have drifted away into a reverie as she was borne aloft on the distant music. I studied her features for a while before I spoke. She was far gone. In that long moment of repose I was struck by how timeless her face was, her profile almost Pre-Raphaelite. Studying her placid expression, I could've painted her from memory just as she appeared at that moment.

"Rocio? Are we still having this conversation?"

Almost startled, she looked at me as if she had suddenly awakened from a light sleep. "That's my neighbor you hear, Berengario de la Peña, playing in the next apartment," she said softly. "Perhaps you remember him just a little? He was a great concert artist in his day. Now he's eighty-two and in poor health. He's waiting to die. I often think that will happen for him at the keyboard one of these days. I know that's what he would want. I can imagine it coming as a crash of discordant notes, the only one he's played in his entire life. It would sound like the sudden ripping of a silk fabric. Then, nothing but silence as he slid to the floor."

I digested this for a moment, thinking more about Edward long buried in the garden. What had he coveted most at his death? The latest object he'd been searching for? For me, it would be the breakthrough painting, the one always waiting out there at the edge of twilight, still beckoning to me after a long session where I hadn't gotten everything quite right. I leaned forward in my chair.

"What was Edward searching for when he died? Was he still on that same quest that drove you away?" It seemed as if I'd been inching toward this for a while. Was she just a bit reluctant to get into it?

Rocio smiled sadly. "Well, yes, I believe he still was, although we never talked about it again after I left. By that time we had certainly discussed it more than enough times. Edward always loved a legend; did you know that about him? He adored it more than the truth or any reality in his life. I think what he loved most about the ancient world was that so much of it has been reduced to myth by the passage of time, which has thrown a veil over it. We can't be that certain about most of it any longer, what it really meant, and more pieces of it are lost every day. Look at what ISIS did in ancient Palmyra. I can only tell you this: when Edward and I separated he was looking for the Veronica, and he believed he was very close to finding it. He had tracked it as far as somewhere in México in the late 1960s or maybe the early 1970s. It may have been in Cuernavaca, I can remember that much. To tell you the truth, I had stopped listening to the saga as much as I might have as we drifted apart toward the end. I was sick of it. They all ended in the same way."

"And what was that?"

"He moved on to something else."

At this final sentence a sharp note crept into her voice, and as she finished, the music abruptly fell silent as if the invisible Berengario's hands had both lifted from the keyboard in surprise, the alignment of his fingers still frozen on that final chord. I stared into the pale golden remnant at the bottom of my almost empty glass, unsure how to respond. Finally I looked up at her again. "Are you telling me that Edward believed the Veronica really exists?"

"Yes. That is exactly what he did believe. While he was far from being a fool, Edward was still capable of believing nearly anything, particularly about himself. For example, he thought all his copied paintings were superior to the originals. That he was improving on the artist's less skillful attempt. He was a great rationalizer."

I found this delusional of Edward, and possibly of Rocio as well if she also ever thought so, and for not thinking he might be a fool because of it. Now I knew why she said Edward had loved legend. His own must have been his favorite.

The Veronica is a cloth or a veil used by a legendary woman of that name who stepped out of the crowd during Christ's walk to the hill of the crucifixion. He had stumbled while carrying the cross on his back. She used this cloth to wipe his face clean of sweat and blood. According to the fable, that image of his face in his final hours had remained imprinted on the fabric. Since then it had been the object of many legends and quests, even figuring in the Crusades. It's also a common subject in many Spanish colonial paintings because of its role in the Stations of the Cross.

"I'm certainly no expert on the Biblical stories," I said, "and I'm not at all a religious person. But I do know the Veronica lore from its many appearances in painting over the centuries, and I don't believe that event is mentioned in any of the Gospels. I've come across the story in several other places and it's a tradition from much later, isn't it? Like from the Middle Ages?"

"I believe you're right, but still, you have to understand that those issues of origin wouldn't have mattered at all to Edward."

"But doesn't that make the Veronica a pious fraud, one of many?"

"Probably." Her tone was light. "But as I said, reality was never what held his attention best. He thought you could go out the door anywhere and find reality on the street or lying in the gutter. It was usually too cheap to be worth his notice. If he did find the original Veronica it would still be nearly a thousand years old, or perhaps even several centuries older than that. What was worth a great deal to Edward was that it had such a long record of veneration, even if it began its existence as a fraud. Like many other things in his life, and in history, it would've been sanctified by the passage of time. Isn't that like the way we want to preserve old buildings, even if they weren't great when they were built? They're simply very old, so we're awed by them. We feel they deserve our reverence and our best efforts to preserve them."

"I see. Other people coveting it must've been part of that too." I was starting to understand the influences in his painting better now. It was not only about superior technique, but equally about his worldview. The approval of others was a major influence on his own opinion. For any copy, I guess the value is no more or less than the merit we assign it. What he was searching for in the Veronica was the oldest, most prestigious fantasy. The one that had drawn the biggest crowds; an article that inspired pilgrimages. Somehow that made sense for him.

"I can see what you're thinking, Paul, that it's all only a lie." There must have been a troubled expression on my face.

I nodded slowly and reluctantly. I didn't want to criticize Edward after his death, and I don't worship the new and the cutting edge, either, but his point of view had never been mine.

"But how rarely," she went on, leaning forward, "is the truth an important part of the dream people spend their lives chasing? That's a concept that belongs more to science, where some things can at least be proven. You and I live in the arts. More than half the time what I write about in my poems is illusion. For me chasing a fantasy doesn't make people stupid or ignorant. I don't write about people I don't respect and sympathize with. Think of the Lost Dutchman Mine, the Fountain of Youth, the Seven Cities of Gold? Think of every person's futile quest, like trying to live a rewarding life with Edward. Think of the search for true love or making great art. Even trying to be a poet. That's what makes people human, starting with me. The truth is out there somewhere, I suppose, but it's not how we live."

"Add life after death to that list," I added with a shrug. Easy for me to say, I was only forty. "That was the charm of Edward, then, was it?"

"And don't forget about the Girl of Your Dreams," she said softly, not answering me directly. "When you are someone's dream girl, it can be hard to measure up to that role all the time. Even half the time."

"Even when you're not half bad," I suggested softly, looking deeper into her dark eyes. I realized I was starting to resonate to her tone a little more than objectivity allowed.

"Thank you." She gave me a wry smile.

"So would you say Edward was kind of a lofty man? There were a couple of times when I thought that, just from talking with him. For my own work, I always look at painting as a craft. I'm not sure he would've said that."

"That's a good way to put it. Still, I will always be sad to see him gone."

"I'm sure. How close was he to getting the Veronica, whatever it might really be?"

"I don't think we'll ever know that, unless you

and your friends can figure it out. I hope you'll tell me if you do. You may find the answer in those journals, if you can get them."

"I think that's now going to be our mission."

Five minutes later, Rocio Valdez placed one of her own slender volumes of poetry face down in my hand as we said goodbye in her doorway. "This is my most recent work."

I thanked her and handed her my business card. "If you think of anything else that might help us please give me a call." Her hand pressed mine when I took it.

My glance didn't stray from her clear and sober eyes for a long moment before I turned away. Deep in thought, I only glanced at the title as I was descending the final step into the courtyard. Her book was titled *An Empty Canvas*. I wasn't surprised to see she was writing in English. My footsteps echoed on the ancient worn paving stones as I skirted the fountain on my way out. Above, somewhere within those lengthy porticoes, the harpsichord had fallen silent again.

I had already passed through the heavy entry doors when the descending sun struck me in the face like a warning from a more hostile era. By the time I entered the blur of Calle San Francisco traffic, I abruptly remembered those two other books at the bottom of the banana box I'd won at the auction. What were they called? Was it *A Painter's Life*? With the shock of Edward's death coming to light before we even left his house that day, I hadn't delved into the box and looked at any of those books again. They were now stored up in my studio, out of sight and untouched inside the cabinet wall.

Pausing on the stone curb, I opened Rocio's book to the title page. It was inscribed, *To Paul Zacher, From my insights to yours, Rocio Valdez*. I wondered if she had been too calm about Edward's murder, even though she said she was reeling. It may only have been her manner.

As I walked thoughtfully down the street toward the jardín, I suddenly realized it was possible that I already owned Edward Jericho's two last journals as well. If we were going to crack this case open, that might well be the way.

CHAPTER SIX

As with the Georges Mazilu painting, now mine, the auctioneers at Bustamante had not paid much attention to Edward's belongings individually. I suppose to an auction cataloguer one lightly used art book looks much like another, and therefore they all went into the art book box in no special order. The used horse books and DVDs went to their own equine box. They felt no other distinctions were necessary. If Edward's two journal volumes had been discovered behind the rest of his art books as Rocio Valdez suggested, then they would simply have fallen forward to announce themselves when the front ones were pulled off the shelf. I recalled no more than that they were quite plain in appearance. The title on both had been artfully designed to resemble hand lettering. Maybe it really was; but I had only glanced at them briefly. In a box where all the other books were large format and bore covers showing the best of the color illustrations from within, they would have drawn no one's eye beyond having the word *Painter* in a pleasant script on the cover.

On my return home from seeing Rocio, I found myself oddly reluctant to start the search for the journals. If the two smaller volumes in the book box really were Edward's life story, they could wait till morning. Whatever they were, Edward wasn't coming back and they wouldn't be likely to tell me who the murderer was. It was almost as if I suspected they were full of things I didn't want to know. I uncorked a bottle of wine, and Maya and I adjourned to the loggia, where I briefed her on Edward's history. Then, with some degree of relief, we talked about the emotional life of horses until the evening chill collected around us and drove us inside.

Back in my studio the following morning I pulled the book box out of my wall of storage cabinets where it rested among rolls of coarse canvas, bundles of wooden stretchers, and assorted props. There was that parcel of new brushes someone had brought me down from the States. This storage area was a source of both developing dreams and lingering memories. I saw the dark blue choker the delectable Barbara Watt had worn when I painted her nude during our first case. I had come closer to getting involved with her than any other, except for the striking itinerant Colombian singer, Yasmin Montoya.

Yasmin had never let me paint her so there were no props from that encounter. Hanging on the clothes bar at the end was the *tejuana* costume Maya had worn when I painted her as Frida Kahlo. That was a picture neither of us wanted to sell, and it still hangs over the fireplace in our great room. Delgado had never understood how I had made her eyebrows join in the center. It doesn't help to tell a literal-minded person that I can paint things that aren't there.

I pulled out the book box from the bottom shelf and went through it in much more detail than I had before the auction. Pacing myself with a kind of building anticipation I couldn't have expressed any clear reason for, I first found individual spaces for the reference books in my small bookcase, and only then took a seat with the journals. Within seconds I knew what I had. There would be no need to email a query to Dillon Gericault in New Orleans.

Both volumes of *A Painter's Life* were written in a dense, neat, and legible hand—how unlike that of an artist! They had been scripted by a person who took pleasure in longhand and knew he had a discernible style. My own penmanship had always been crabbed and approximate, and was now largely fallen out of use. At this point in my life I can hardly do any more in cursive than to scrawl my name on a check. I couldn't help but admire Edward for having made a minor art of a skill so private and unfashionable. It said something about him.

Both volumes opened with a date rather than

a title page or any introduction, which made me think that although they were labeled Vol. I & II, there must have been earlier sections in this saga. Had Edward started a new numbering sequence after some significant event? Like B. V. and A. V., before and after he started chasing the Veronica? The earlier of the two opening entries was dated in the summer more than five years before. It plunged right into the action:

June 23

Now I'm sure that Pedro of Aragon saw some version of the Veronica in Rome in 1439. The main question for me is which version that was, because by that time copying the Artifact was already common. In the material from *Archivos Estatales de España* I came across this in his travel journals (now translated from the archaic Spanish and digitized, thank God!):

"On the choir side of the altar of the Santo Hilario stands a pillar as high as the ceiling, one of four that support the dome. Preserved within a niche near the top is the Holy Veronica. During the times when it is to be shewn to the people a door is opened at the edge of the dome and a device like a chair is let down by means of ropes. Borne in this device is a canon of the church, and when he has been lowered the proper distance, he removes the gilded coffer. Whereupon he raises the Sacred Veronica from its enclosure and reveals it unto the gathered worshippers outside who have made sojourn there at that hour. Many times the faithful fear for their lives, so many are in attendance, and so great is the press of flesh in their eagerness for eternal salvation."

Here there opened a small blank space on the page as Edward changed to his own reaction to reading this. It was easy to imagine him bent over this first volume.

So even then the fervor was already part of it. This version has the right stuff. Pedro died in 1486, so he is no more than a credible source, an eyewitness locating the relic in Rome during his youth. The real question is how and why it left, particularly if it was already such an object of reverence. No one would've been willing to part with it except under extreme duress. And as we know, the duress was coming.

Rocio will love to hear about this tonight at dinner! Her poetry often reveals a taste for mystery, which makes her a great partner in my search.

I wondered how she would've responded to that

final line. Since I already knew how things had ended with Rocio, I reserved judgment on it. In the pages that followed I found more entries of this kind, suggesting that Edward's research had been wide-ranging and detailed. It made me wonder, as a working painter, why he had been willing to devote so much time to it. I again recalled Rocio saying his productivity was even compromised during the later part of their time together. On these pages he never held back from making his own observations on what he'd found. Often his notes comprised a commentary on a commentary. I placed a bookmark at that entry and moved on through some unrelated material on paint suppliers in Mexico City and why several of them didn't deserve to live.

Here I was interrupted by the phone. I fished it out of my pocket. It was Diego Delgado calling with the autopsy results.

"So kind of you to offer me this information," I said, after the usual round of courtesies. I knew more about his kids than I did about any of my own cousins, but then, I hadn't come from a Mexican family, and my parents weren't close to their siblings.

"You will not be surprised from this," he said, "but the death of Eduardo Hericho was of a knife wound struck from behind. Three upper ribs on the left side show the marks from it."

"So then does that suggest two strikes of the

knife? One entering to mark the two adjacent ribs and the other marking only one?"

"I believe that is so, yes."

"And does the fact that they were both on the left suggest a left handed person was the killer?"

"That is what I also think, from my experience."

"Anything more?"

"Little more except that the condition of the body is correct for remaining in the ground during fourteen months, *mas o menos*, more or less."

"Do you think a having a look at the teeth or a DNA test might be a good idea here? Edward's brother is still alive for comparison."

"Señor Zacher, this is México where we are all living. Señor Hericho has been gone fourteen months. This is a corpse wearing his watch that has had fourteen months in the ground on his property. What more do you wish than this? You would like us to be the FBI? I can show you our annual budget downtown if you wish."

"I see your point."

"Thank you. But now I have a question for you."

"Go ahead."

"There is someone employing you and the Paul Zacher Agency to investigate this crime?"

"No. We are doing this for the public good, as you might say. Anything we discover we will turn over to you with no credit to ourselves." My eyes avoided looking at the two journal volumes on my lap as I said this. I rose and set them on the small table next to me. If I gave them to the Judicial Police they would vanish into their murky evidence storage system, never to be seen again. Besides, there was more to this case than Edward's murder. You would've thought Delgado had more recent, and therefore, more pressing cases to look at.

"So it could not be suggested by anyone that the Paul Zacher Agency lacks confidence in the Judicial Police?"

"Not at all!" In saying this, I knew my voice was too loud. "We are assisting you just as your office has so often assisted us on our cases that were not directly related to a judicial enquiry." Trying to think of one where that was true, I came up with nothing. "The murder of a gringo is always of serious concern to the Judicial Police, as we both know. Of course it is no more important than the death of any Mexican in this town, but the publicity across the border is so much worse. I know the mayor's office and the business community both hate that."

"Exactly."

"And I also heard you had a directive from the new mayor to keep a lid on crimes like this," I said, "since they discourage tourism and investment."

"Indeed. If only we could keep a lid on them. Such an expressive phrase to have in English."

"So there we are. You and I find ourselves on the same side of the border once again." Even so, I could detect the vestiges of a frown in his silence as I waited a long moment for him to respond. "So is there more?"

"Well, possibly. I can share this with you since you are so helpful and we are now of a team. Late last evening a break-in occurred at the home of Neil and Louise Wilson. By the grace of God they were not at home. They live on Umaran, a block or so from Zacateros, I believe. Do you know them?"

"Only by sight. I think they were at the auction on Saturday." The Wilson house was not far from where I sat as we talked.

"Yes. They bought the dining table and chairs of our murder victim," he said.

"OK." I recalled seeing them. I pictured a long pine plank table in good condition with eight matching chairs bearing seats upholstered with a fabric woven in an indigenous pattern that might have been Oaxacan. The set had a not quite antique look, more like vintage mid century. The structure was blocky and straightforward. "Were they stolen?" This made no sense to me. How often does a burglar pull up on a narrow street with a moving van at night?

"No, but they were vandalized. The fabric on the chair seats was cut through in each case, on all the chairs, going around the edge. So it could be lifted."

"That's odd, isn't it? It must have been only a search for something." Did the intruder think Edward had hidden the Veronica inside a chair seat, where people would park their butts on it, and do worse, after a lot of pork gravy and other rich sauces like mole? And what about the stress of bearing that much weight on an ancient filmy piece of material? Most chair seats are not solid; they're made of cushioned fabric over webbing interleaved between four frame members. This burglar was not thinking clearly. Maybe he was only desperate. But why?

"Yes, so it seems. What do you think they might have been looking for there, Señor Zacher, if you should want to risk a guess? Are chair seats a typical place for gringos to hide their valuables?"

"Like money? That's what I would've been looking for. Painters often come up a bit short at the end of the month."

"Perhaps. In any case, I will leave you now to your good work. Paint more nudes, and in the meantime, if you think of something else, please to let me know."

"Of course. Como siempre. As always." Since our first case Delgado had never recovered from the fact that people would pose nude for me, hour after hour.

I sat down for a moment to think about the burglary, since I had once again found myself pacing as I talked to Delgado. Lying in the bottom of the art book box was the Bustamante receipt from the auction. Naturally I had kept it to deduct the expense on my income taxes. I picked it up and punched in their number in Querétaro, forty minutes away, where after two rings a young woman answered.

I introduced myself and told her I had been at the Jericho household auction in San Miguel, and what a great job I thought they had done. I could see where I might use them myself some day. She didn't respond, sensing, perhaps, exactly what kind of boilerplate introduction that was.

"I'm also wondering whether it is possible to obtain a list of people who had the winning bids. There were one or two lots where I wanted to make a higher offer to the buyer." I had never done this but it seemed plausible that someone might.

"Oh no, Señor Zacher, I am very sorry. For the security of the buyer we do not release that information to the public."

"Well, that seems odd, because I heard that someone had gotten a copy of that list." This was only a guess on my part, but how else to explain the break in at the Wilsons? There could've been a witness at the auction, but he probably wouldn't have known the winning bidders or where they lived. Lots were knocked down to a number on a paddle, not a name.

A moment of silence followed. "Here at the

Bustamante we have a strict policy, *señor*, to protect our clients. The person who gave out that list was fired for that violation."

"I understand, and I support that. Can you tell me his name?"

"Oh no, Señor Zacher, we do not release that kind of information from our employees either."

"Thank you."

Given their failure to research and assign estimated values to the Jericho lots, I thought they might have other reasons for confidentiality as well.

I sat in my silent studio for a while with the developing sensation that I had stumbled into a larger situation than I first imagined. Even though Edward had been gone fourteen months, this was still not a cold case. The person who had gotten the successful auction bidders' list may have been innocent in his curiosity. Or, more likely, he might have heard about Edward's quest for the Veronica and believed the artist had been successful in finding it. The constant problem with pursuing an object of great value is that the searcher often has to publicize his interest in it by asking questions, which provokes other people's interest. Rocio didn't think he'd found it, but she had dropped out of Edward's life six months before his disappearance. What had happened in the interval? Perhaps the journals would tell me more.

As I sat there thinking, the Mazilu painting, *Ma-*

donna in a Venetian Costume, again caught my eye. It was the only picture by another artist I had ever hung in my own studio, which suggests how I felt about it. How odd I had thought that on his return I might be selling it back to Edward for what I paid for it; $2150 was probably a quarter or less of what it was worth.

I had hung the Mazilu above a small desk where I set up my laptop when I need it in the studio. I put it there to keep visitors from getting close enough to put their hands on the delicate canvas. I had seen people reach toward it at the auction, but perhaps knowing its appeal, Edward had hung it slightly out of reach. It was a fine, if rather subtle, piece of work. The Madonna stared pensively, but knowingly out at me. I wondered for a moment, after she'd been hanging on Edward's wall for so long, what it was she knew that I didn't. Had she witnessed his death? From my own biased perspective, as a mature work of art her image was of more value than the Veronica, which could hardly be any more than a fanciful but ancient unsigned copy of an original that had never existed.

Perhaps the slashing of eight fabric chair seats in the Wilsons' dining room meant nothing, but the range of what it could have meant, coming as it did right after the auction, was too narrow to ignore. I chose to think that the Veronica was in play because I couldn't come up with any other explanation. Of course, my name was on that successful bidders list too, as was Maya's. Perhaps it was time to set a trap for the other seekers, although the trick, of course, as always in this business, was to avoid being trapped ourselves.

On the lamp table by my side was also Rocio's slender chapbook of poetry, the one she'd given me as I left, *An Empty Canvas*. Who was she, really? Perhaps this would tell me, or at least give me a hint. I opened it to a page at random about halfway through.

> *Tell me, then, which way blows the wind,*
> *When the leaves don't fall*
> *When the feather drops like a stone*
> *Tell me, then, which way the fire burns when it dies.*
> *When the ash grows cold*
> *When love withers in your eyes*
> *Tell me, then, why days are shorter now,*
> *Why nights go on in silence*
> *Until the dawn, until the dawn.*

Thinking that the two identical halves of the final line had completely different meanings, I closed the book there, placed both journal volumes in the table drawer, and gazed out the window onto Quebrada for a while.

CHAPTER SEVEN

Returning to the journals after a distracted painting session, I felt I was ready to see how the search ended, not that I thought it ever had. Opening to the final inscribed page of the second volume, I was surprised to find this entry:

October 24

"The most holy tabernacle wherein the divine Relic of Veronica is kept is wrought of the finest Greek workmanship, and the design, also wrought all in silver, is of the most ancient character. The legend on the scroll that accompanies it describes the manner of its passage back from the sack of Constantinople in 1204 in the company of Venetian Crusaders. In the following year, they bore it in sacred pilgrimage to Rome, and presented it in a private ceremony on the floor of the old St. Peter's to Pope Innocentius Tertius."

This seemed to be drawn from closer to the middle of the search, rather than the end. The date was approximately three weeks before Edward's disappearance, but no one could say for certain. Still, there was no reason to think the quest had been completed when Edward died, rather than simply interrupted. I read the passage again and derived no more sense of closure from it. So far in my journey through the journals I had observed no codes or hidden messages.

In our terms today we call this Pope Innocent III, which had to be a difficult name to live up to, then as now. Perhaps it was more like a stage name. Edward identified no author for this segment, as if he very well knew who had written it and saw no need to remind himself. Or, it may have been truly anonymous in the record. It slowly became clearer to me that these journals had been penned for his exclusive use. He would have been astounded to imagine me or anyone else sitting there reading them after his death.

Still, unattributed as this excerpt was, I couldn't help but see the logic of it. Descended from Constantine's fourth century change of capital cities, the Byzantine emperors were the successors to the Romans, until Constantinople itself fell to the Ottoman Turks in 1453. That same misguided Fourth Crusade of 1204 had sent the Eastern Empire into a slow but irreversible decline.

But any number of pious copies of the Veronica

could easily have been painted under that old regime in Constantinople, since Rome was a turgid backwater during most of this period. Although the Popes had remained in the city when Christianity split into two groups between east and west (aside from most of the fourteenth century when the western popes resided in Avignon), Rome was only the shabby core of a ruined and exhausted empire. It must have been a depressing place to live, with marble being salvaged from the ancient buildings and recut for more mundane construction, or simply burned to produce lime to make cement. Only the advent of the Renaissance finally gave the Eternal City a reason to stand up and move forward again. This renewed sense of pride came not from the Church, but from a rediscovery of the city's ancient arts and history.

One aspect I was finding difficult about the Jericho journals as I continued to work through them was that Edward had simply collected the passages in the order he came across them, as you would expect from writing them down day by day. That made sense, but he had made no attempt later to sort and organize the material in a sequence that would tell the story coherently to an outsider who was more interested in the information apart from his personal life's journey, which I was still trying to avoid. If one entry spoke of the events of 1279, the next could focus on 1146 or 1490. Or there might be interspersed a segment on linen weaving in the Holy

Land during the first century of this era. They badly needed an editor, because the entire story was organized only in one vulnerable and now inaccessible place, the mind of Edward Jericho.

Worse, and this should have been no surprise either, the material was constantly interspersed with other events in his personal life. I could understand that he gave a great deal of space over to painting, particularly the mastering and polishing of certain effects from the artists he was copying. But for myself, I had no use for this. In fact, I actively wanted to avoid it. For me the interest in copying another artist's work lay in discovering how it was done by working it out myself, possibly repeating the same series of errors that artist had made in getting there originally. I didn't want to see a manual that gave the secrets away with no effort on my part. Where was the challenge in that?

More disturbing were the passages on Rocio Valdez and their failed relationship, some of them quite emotional and sensitive. This was the part of it that was farthest from being any business of mine, even though I was a professional snoop. She had made a point of telling me she'd never looked into the journals, although she had observed where Edward kept them. When I heard this I regarded it as a standard boilerplate disclaimer. It may have been true, but anyone in her position would say that. In the months near the end when their relationship was breaking down, could she really have never yielded to the impulse to look into them and find out what Edward was thinking, as opposed to what he was telling her?

I honestly tried not to skim through this material, but certain key words flew out at me unasked as I flipped through the pages. One statement I noted in three or four places was that he felt Rocio had the most beautiful breasts he had ever seen. He also stated in several entries that he was willing to interrupt his obsession with copying other people's work if she would only pose nude for him, but she always refused. If in these lines he never recorded the reasons for her rejection of this request, it may have only been because she didn't tell him why. It could have been no more complicated than simple modesty, a typical attitude of most Mexican women.

I settled back in my chair as I reread this and then set the volume closed in my lap. It made me feel conflicted. Maya had posed nude for me in more than forty paintings, so I could appreciate his frustration with having an unwilling model of great potential so close to him. But that was only one aspect of their relationship among many others. I also felt that since Rocio was a poet of some distinction, Edward was failing to emphasize other important features of her character, particularly of her mental and creative life. Other than at the beginning of their affiliation, I had seen few references in the journals to her literary efforts, although I hadn't spent much time looking. It was not germane to the case, and his view of it was irrelevant now.

Another way to look at this was that Rocio, at least, was occupied with completely original writing of her own, while Edward sat at his easel copying the work of others, even as he felt superior to them. A poem is just as valid and unique as a painting, but unlike what Edward was doing, no one would ever copy a poem word for word and think it was an achievement, even better than the original. Maybe this was the reason he didn't spend much effort recognizing her artistic output. Had she been a bit threatening to him without intending to?

What I was faced with in scanning these two volumes was the usual executor's task of deciding what was worth keeping and what should be destroyed. As a person more visual than literary, it was a burden I didn't care to take on. I decided to forward the two journal volumes to Dillon once the case was finished. I hadn't seen anything so far that would've helped Diego Delgado, and he would've had no way to know they existed if neither I nor Rocio told him.

That same day Maya and I received an informal email notice from Dillon Gericault giving a tentative date for a memorial service and an invitation to speak if we wished. I knew it was coming. By that time the mostly skeletal remains from the garden had been cremated and the service was scheduled for less than two weeks out. Edward's urn was to be placed in a niche in the quieter, expat section of the Panteón. There had been no question of this since he had specified it in his will, which Dillon had been keeping. He had furnished Delgado with a copy, and the *licenciado* was keeping us posted. Through a local burial society, the niche and cremation had already been paid for long before his most recent and ultimate disappearance. Even at forty-five, it was almost as if Edward Jericho had sensed some uncertainty about his future.

What the journals were going to require was a thorough examination of each entry, and I wasn't ready for that. I turned back to a page I had landed on that was dated only about eight months before his disappearance, which was two months before he and Rocio parted. This was all in Edward's own voice.

Apr. 9

The saddest part of this story may well be the two surviving fragments of an eyewitness account of how the Veronica was being passed from hand to hand in a Roman tavern in 1527, the year the city was sacked by the forces of the Emperor Charles V. This is the part that is the most painful for me to contemplate—the idea of the Holy Relic in the grubby hands of apostates and unbelievers only there to attack the Pope. I am truly shocked that it somehow survived in the condition it's in today. The task now is to find who had it next.

The page and the entry both ended there, and on the next leaf, dated two days later, Edward offered a rebuttal to Rocio's recent argument that he had become obsessed with the Veronica. The timing of this entry suggests that perhaps he had shown her that much of what he'd found. One does not characterize a deep engagement with recovering a historic relic as an obsession, he declared in his opening. To me that sounded a bit pretentious, as if he identified with Howard Carter and Lord Carnarvon in their 1922 discovery of the tomb of Tutankhamen. He felt the word had inappropriate emotional overtones, and went on to explain and amplify what our proper sense of custodianship of the past ought to be. For a variety of reasons this also reminded me of Rocio's comment on Edward's lack of interest in reality.

Nevertheless my blood had literally run cold at the last two sentences for the ninth of April. The clear implication was that Edward had direct knowledge of what condition the artifact had survived in. Even if he hadn't managed to obtain possession of the Veronica, Edward must have at least *seen* it, and possibly even held it in his own hands. Might this have been too much reality for him?

Maya and I had a long conversation in bed that night about the journals, particularly the final line of the April 9th entry. Her lifelong family–inspired antireligious stance made her position less sanguine than mine on issues like this. Had the Veronica been autographed by Christ with a Montblanc fountain pen as he got up again from his fall and staggered on toward Golgotha, she still would not have assigned it much value. While I wasn't a believer either, I gave it more credence just from its historical context.

"I think Edward died for it," I said. "That's what gives the Veronica value and meaning to me. I also think it might be in play again now, although the journals haven't confirmed that." I had already told her at breakfast about the Winslows' set of eight slashed chair seats.

"Paul, I know we said we'd look into this. I'm sure Rocio is hoping for something important from us, some breakthrough that the police can't produce. But let's not get too involved with it, OK? After all this time we can't bring Edward back, and I don't think we're ever going to come across an artifact like that, and he couldn't either. He was only fooling himself. If people have been searching for it for a thousand years, it's not just suddenly going to show up on a Sunday afternoon at the flea market in San Miguel. Don't you think that Edward might have been a little…*light* in the skepticism department?"

"I can see where you would think he was too

credulous. Maybe I've thought that myself at times. But I tend to make excuses for people who try important things, who're willing to stretch their boundaries even when they stumble. And you can't deny that Edward could tackle the style of almost any painter."

Maya raised a single finger in the air. "Except his own." Her head was cocked over her left shoulder and her lips were pursed. She has a way of sticking a hatpin through some of my statements, no matter how profound.

"Yes, I know, but even so. That was still no small challenge."

"OK, then, but I'll still say this. He was what I think of as, and this is a new word I just learned, woo-woo. Painting all those filmy Victorian ladies with the hint of a nipple standing up under the sheer fabric? He was never able to do a hard-edged nude the way you like to do. To tell you the truth, I'm not sure what Rocio ever saw in him. Maybe you can get her to tell you. I think she wants to be your buddy."

There was no disagreeing with this, not that my nudes had many hard edges, although maybe a few appeared on the teeth in good light. But Maya wasn't finished.

"Paul, this is going to sound unkind, OK? Edward was a lightweight dreamer, and we shouldn't be surprised if he got in over his depth. He didn't care for reality the way most of us do, the way most of us *have to*. What would've helped was if someone had taken him outside and shaken him up a bit. Pushed him against the wall until he felt more anchored. I don't know if Rocio Valdez ever had it in her to do that. She would rather write a poem about it. She has too many soft edges, the kind he liked best."

I didn't say anything in response to this.

"Maybe you like her soft edges too," she added, not looking at me.

I believe there was a time in my early youth when I thought women were sentimental, but I cannot now recall exactly when that was.

Much later, when I was mostly asleep and drifting through a shimmery field of orange chiffon gowns and neoclassical furnishings, all rendered with exquisite brushwork, I realized I had entered a strangely familiar Edward Jericho period fantasy trip that wasn't altogether comfortable. My extended fingers traveled over a few notes of the keyboard of a dreamland harpsichord nearby, but it shied away at my touch. Was it only Maya's ribs? At that moment my cell phone went off within reach of my pillow, a foolish place to keep it, and one I've regretted in the past. Any call at two in the morning is never good news, but I picked it up anyway.

"Paul! Paul! It's Rocio Valdez. There is someone

in my apartment! Can you help me? The street door is never locked. Just push it open!" Her voice was muffled as if she were still in bed, hiding beneath the covers. No help with concealment there. That telltale lump was the first place the intruder would look.

The connection was abruptly broken off as they always seem to be when you need more information, and I heard nothing else from her as I threw my legs over the side of the bed. It was a frigid night and we hadn't lit the bedroom fireplace earlier. When my feet hit the floor I wished I still had pajamas with feet.

Maya sat up, pulling her hair out of her eyes.

"It's Rocio. She's got an intruder." Maya said nothing, but reflexively reached into her nightstand drawer for her gun.

I pulled on my jeans and shirt, slipped my gun into my belt, and after a lot of rings reached Cody three minutes later as I ran out the door. I could taste a sour note in my throat as I climbed into the van out on the dimly lit cobblestones of Quebrada. The steering wheel and controls were shockingly cold to my touch. Somewhere down the street, but high above as if on a third floor rooftop, a dog was barking and howling in what sounded like abject terror.

I'm coming, I'm coming now, I'm on the way, I said to both myself and to Rocio Valdez.

CHAPTER EIGHT

Ripping through the empty city like a comic book hero in a battered denim jacket, I arrived at the old mansion on Calle San Francisco at about 2:15. Although I could've used his armed support, I had decided not to wait at home for Cody to join me, since he had a little farther to travel. A lot of Mexicans don't trust the police, so that might have explained why Rocio chose to call me. Still, I wasn't thrilled to be acting as a one-man untrained and unpaid police force on duty 24/7, but what could I do? The woman's life was at risk and we were already tracking one killer in the case. You always have to go where it takes you, because once you're in, you're in all the way.

Traffic on the busy street where she lived had dropped to nothing more than the intermittent taxi idling at the stand across the way, its driver waiting for someone to stagger out of a bar and forget where he had left his car. I pulled up directly in front of Rocio's entry, a feat impossible during the day. With only one or two cars parked further on up the street, no one on foot was in view. The front door was open a few inches as if positioned that way by someone who didn't wish to be slowed down by any obstacles as he rushed out with a fragile sacred relic in his hand. The obvious option was to wait there and shoot him as he came out, but the Zacher Agency is usually more subtle than that. There was probably no other exit to the building.

On the other hand, Rocio Valdez was apparently upstairs alone with the intruder and Edward had been murdered. I wanted to catch this guy in the act before he did her any harm. I rushed inside the weathered mesquite doors with my gun drawn. The shadowy edges of the stone railings on the second floor were barely visible. The first floor ceilings must have been six meters high, and the staircases at both corners had a landing midway up where they reversed direction. In the center of the courtyard I could just make out the profile of the massive fountain, now silent and somehow sinister at this hour.

I found myself growing more angry as I inched toward the stairs. No one had opted out of this Jericho tragedy more firmly than Rocio had. Twenty months had passed since she parted from him. The prominent cause of her exit had been this same senseless quest that was now driving me and the rest of the Paul Zacher Agency to take to the streets. The irony of this was not lost on me, and while Rocio was back in the middle of it again,

I now felt like the heir to an old vendetta. I didn't know that for certain, but what else could it be? Perhaps killing Edward had not been enough.

Then I thought of something else. What if the person who'd gotten the successful bidder list from Bustamante Estate Auctions was working from the back section forward? I couldn't guess why, but the Wilsons had been hit first. Rocio was a Valdez. It was an exact back to front progression. That wasn't logical as we would normally think of it, but it did not escape me that on any list starting from the back, Zacher would've been a no-brainer as the first move. I had lived with this in school all my academic life, often knowing the answer first and getting called on last. Why were they avoiding me? And then I had a second thought. Was it a coincidence that I had been summoned away from my own house in the middle of the night?

Maya was now home alone, but she had long known the Agency drill. As I dressed she had drawn her gun out of the nightstand without comment and slid off the safety. This was her standard practice when I was called away on an active case, and tonight was not the first time. I knew she would not be sleeping now until I returned. At least she was armed and alert. I also knew from experience that she was not a bad shot. Although she didn't mind griping about cases now and then, when the action heated up she didn't rattle easily, and she was reliable without question, as much as any of us were.

The only light within the old casa came from the chancy night sky viewed through a half dozen glass panels high over the courtyard. It wasn't much, only enough to move around in without walking into anything, but not enough to hold a formal shootout. I heard no sound. Still, my mouth was getting drier by the moment, a sure sign of impending action. Careful to muffle the echo of my footsteps on the stone pavers, I headed for the staircase opposite the one I'd used on my earlier visit to climb to the second level. My heart was already beating too fast to permit careful thinking.

Halfway up, as I was changing direction to the second level, the light from the street door opened a wider arc on the floor. An oversize figure with one arm extended came crouching through with a hostile profile. In two steps he quickly faded from view against the blackness of the adjacent wall. This had to be Cody.

I couldn't call out to summon him without putting a target on myself, and I didn't know whether he'd seen me. Probably he hadn't, but at least he would've noticed my van parked at the door. He did not know which apartment Rocio lived in. I had told him it was number three when I woke him up as I left the house, but how could he see which one that was when he got inside? It's not as if the apartments all had lighted doorbells. The unit numbers were on tiny ceramic tablets near the door handle. The only way to see them was if he had his miniscule flashlight with him and he could shine it on the wall, hiding the glow with both hands.

Reaching the door of apartment number three, in the near total darkness under the portico I couldn't see that it was standing open until I was only a few steps away. No sound issued from further within as I stepped forward with my gun ready. I knew I was in the big reception room where Rocio and I had talked before, and I could remember where most of the furniture was. I couldn't imagine where she might be hiding. No lights appeared to be on anywhere. Standing away from the doorway, I hesitated, straining to hear the slightest noise.

"Paul," Cody's voice whispered at the doorframe after a long moment had passed.

"Come on in." I waved back at him but I knew he couldn't see my gesture. His small penlight came alive and feebly swept the corners of the room, finally catching my feet. He moved it away and kept it at arm's length so anyone shooting at it would only be firing at his hand, a mercifully smaller target than Cody himself. In three nearly silent steps he was next to me. With my gun extended, I kept listening as if both our lives were at stake, but there was absolutely no sound to hear.

"I think there's no one here," he whispered as he moved toward the kitchen. In a moment he came out again. I couldn't hear him shrug. "Have they got her?

Could they have taken her away? How could they get past you?"

"I don't know. Maybe before I got here?"

We both crept toward the bedroom, even though I didn't think any intruder would still be there waiting for us. I switched on the bedside lamp. That room was empty too. The bedclothes were hurled over the side as if Rocio had leaped up in panic. On the floor next to the bed and pointing toward the pillow, a single cream-colored satin slipper had been left behind. It suggested a struggle not so much lost as only launched in a moment of wild confusion and unresolved. The adjacent bathroom with its 1930s fixtures was also empty, the door standing open. So where was she? The bedroom window overlooking the courtyard was too high off the floor to offer any access without a ladder, and both rooms had a skylight but no other visible exits.

The apartment held only those three major rooms. Could Rocio have fled to a neighbor? Wouldn't every one of their doors be locked and bolted at this hour? Had she fled for help to the aged Berengario de la Peña? She'd said he was waiting to die, but it wouldn't have been in defending her.

As if someone had been taking a rather chilly public bath at that unexpected moment, the sound of a voluminous splash hitting the stone floor in the courtyard pulled both of us to attention. Cody got out through the entry before I did, because I was still searching for the light switch. What we both saw below was the phantom of a drenched man, barely lit at the back, bolting through the now wide-open entry, still streaming water as he emerged under the street lights of Calle San Francisco. The glow spilling through the doorway traced the soaked track of his passage all the way back to the fountain in the center of the enclosure.

That was where he had listened to us, or watched us, at least, as we both came in, interrupting his flight. He must have been freezing to death and had reached his limit.

My first instinct was to chase the intruder, but Cody seized my arm. "Let's find Rocio first. That's why we're here," he said in a normal tone. He often made me wonder what normal was for him. I turned back and my hand finally found the light switch. As it went on a door appeared in the back wall of the reception room. It simply opened from a place where no door had existed a moment before. The narrow profile of the opening perfectly fit the framed contours of the vertical wall paneling, as if the entire wall was composed of a series of undetectable doors with rails between them.

"Thank you both for coming," Rocio said, gathering a pale blue robe about her. She also wore a single slipper and carried a candle. "Thank God for these concealed staff passages. This one runs from the kitchen to the bedroom."

"The maid could serve the madam without going through the salon," I said. I had seen them before, mostly in Europe, but it made sense that an elegant old mansion here would also be laid out this way.

I introduced Cody as my partner in the Agency. She disappeared for a moment and returned still in the robe but wearing both slippers. She had also pulled her hair into some order.

"Are you all right?" Cody said. His eyes scanned her, and then the delicate furniture behind her.

She nodded. "Only scared to death." She disappeared into the dark kitchen and a moment later returned with a blocky chair for Cody. "Now let's talk." She looked down at the upholstery in surprise as she set it down. "The burglar cut up this for some reason."

"Was that from Edward's house?"

"Right. We had this chair and two others with a small table in the kitchen there. It matches the dining room set. He gave this to me when I left, since he would never eat in that kitchen."

"Then I think you'll find that the other two were slashed as well," I said.

Cody went over and examined the apartment door lock. "This is an older piece, an antique, really. I wouldn't put much confidence in it. Doesn't it use a skeleton key? I'd start using this as back up until I had a more modern lock put in." He pointed at a bolt that went from the bottom of the door into the floor.

"You're right," she said. "I don't know why I felt secure here, but thank you both so much for coming over at this hour."

Cody gave her a paternal smile. "Can you tell us why you didn't also call the police?"

What he meant was, why did you call us at all? Having the police and the Agency converge on this scene simultaneously was likely to get someone killed.

"Is there a trust issue here?" I said.

"Well, you could say that, I guess. Licenciado Delgado believes that I murdered Edward."

We both looked at her in shock. I had noticed that Rocio Valdez was left-handed, but I liked to think Delgado would need more than that to hang the crime on her shoulders. He couldn't have recovered much in forensic evidence from the burial. Nothing I had seen so far in the journals suggested she had a motive. Edward had never felt any threat from her, at least in what I had read so far, but there was still a lot of material that remained to be covered.

"What did you see?" said Cody, quite calmly, although he didn't reach for his notepad.

"Nothing at all, I only heard someone come in. Those door hinges squeak a little, and I've never oiled them because I always told myself that was my security system. I haven't ever thrown that old rusty floor bolt. I can hardly stand to touch it, but now I will."

"And when you called me at home, where were you?"

"I was already inside that passageway I came out of just now. I could hear him moving around in the kitchen and in this room, but he never discovered where I was. I'm hoping he thought I wasn't home."

I could imagine her terror, and I felt my sympathy flare up for her as a woman alone and under attack. "Would you like to come home with me now?" I said.

"Not tonight, Paul, but I have had worse offers than that." She managed a grin. Some of her spirit was reviving.

"I meant that Maya and I have a spare bedroom. Cody doesn't."

"I know. I'll be OK." She smiled and placed her hand over mine for a brief moment.

Chatting about other things for a while to lighten the mood, Cody and I stayed with Rocio long enough to see her calmed down and ready to go back to bed. We paused to listen outside as she turned the key and threw the floor bolt behind us. Downstairs we checked the fountain and paced off the periphery of the courtyard before we left.

On the street a ragged and evaporating trail of wet footprints traveled up the pavement in the direction away from the *jardín*. About a dozen meters along it turned and stopped at the curb, as if someone had climbed into a car, soaking wet, and been driven away. We both stepped into the street and stared at the pavers. They were dry.

I pulled out my cell and snapped three photos of the clearest footprints. The light was marginal and the edges of the treads were getting fuzzy, but they might be usable if we ever developed a suspect. In one of them I placed my own foot next to it so we could gauge the size of that shoe against mine.

"Our fountain diver got in from the passenger side." Cody said. "He wasn't the driver."

"Unless it was a pickup with a bench seat in front. He could just slide across."

"Did you notice the vehicle parked there when you came up?"

"No, only that there was one. It could've been a pickup too, I guess. I was thinking about what kind of danger Rocio was in. Did you?"

"No. I was thinking about what kind of danger you were in."

"So we both missed the boat on that detail."

"Anyway, whoever did that invasion was a sap," Cody said. He had his own way of evaluating criminals. Sap was level one, a rank beginner.

"Why is that?"

"What would she have for him, after he went to all that trouble? If he had the list of winning bidders, he would know she had that *tondo* of yours, but nothing more. What good is that?"

"Well, it's of considerable esthetic value."

"I'm talking about where you could put the Veronica if you had it."

"Well, not there."

"Are you getting any of this yet? Do I need to come over for some reading sessions from those journals?"

"Not so far, but I'll tell you when or if that changes."

I dialed Maya to see how things were at home.

CHAPTER NINE

After sleeping late the following morning, I was back sifting through one of the journals during a late breakfast, reading a passage where Edward was airing his opinions and speculations. I wished I had the means of evaluating them without repeating his years of research, but for most of this I was going to take his word for it. After all, it was a pro bono case and nothing was going to bring him back. This segment came from the spring of the year of his disappearance.

April 13

The Volto Santo (the Holy Face), the Sudarium, and the Mandylion of Edessa: These are the principal aliases I was able to find by searching the earliest records.

It is now my belief that the Mandylion of Edessa and the original Veronica are one and the same. First mentioned around 593, one source tells how the Mandylion, the image of Christ's face, was used in 544 in defense of the city of Edessa (in northern Macedonia) against the Persians. Some later attributed the cloth to a court painter, but with little detail and no substantiation. (I merely mention this for accuracy.) The image was moved in the tenth century to Constantinople, possibly for safety during the growing threat from the Turks. This was implicit, but unstated. That would fit with some earlier accounts of the Venetian Crusaders taking it away with them in 1204.

I flipped ahead through two similar pages of late classical speculation until I found this:

Why would Rocio be trying to force me into making a choice...?

A long passage followed that was highlighted by a dozen underlined words and five or six exclamation points. So this was where it started to come apart for them. I didn't read all of it, closing the book without marking my place, and considering for a while whether or when I should tell Rocio I had found the two journal volumes. Perhaps I would soon, but not just yet.

I went back upstairs to resume a landscape I was working on. At about eleven Maya appeared in the doorway of the studio, her arms folded. Normally she would've been gone by then.

"You're not riding today?" I said, looking up without setting down my brush. She was wearing her normal spray-on jeans and a snug knit top.

"Later. I'm thinking about stopping at Rancho Aria for a conversation on my way."

"Do you think they can add something to this?" I paused with my brush in the air. We had finished our recent investigation there in a bad odor with the owners, even though we'd solved the case, the one we filed as *Uneasy Rider*.

"My idea was that since Max is dead now, Phaedra might be willing to talk to me about Edward's time boarding his horse there. You recall how rigid Max was about his image." Max Kingman, the owner of Rancho Aria, had for decades been confined to a wheelchair after a jumping accident in his youth. Only shortly before his death did he unexpectedly regain his power of movement. All through his immobile years he had portrayed himself as the ultimate critic of equestrian talents in others that he no longer possessed himself.

"It's up to you, but you might get her to talk. I would start by making her understand that you don't blame her for selling Edward's Azteca stallion to pay his board bill. That's always a tough spot for the ranch owner to be left in when the monthly cash flow stops. Even so, some riders are still sensitive about it."

"Of course. Do you want to come along? You don't have to, I know you're still working."

I sat back in my chair. "Thanks for asking, but I think I'd probably inhibit her responses. When I talked to her before it always seemed like she was afraid I might see through her." I offered nothing more, although I couldn't think of anyone who didn't see through her. Anyway, Maya didn't need my prompting; she already knew exactly who and what Phaedra was.

Now in her early fifties, Phaedra Montgomery was a British actress who had specialized in playing upper class women. Born in poverty in London's East End as Thelma Mae Perkins (Cody's research connections had unearthed this), she came to the theater after winning a teen beauty contest. Once she had made her mark on the West End stage, she continued the charade of aristocratic lineage into her private life when she married Max Kingman, who came from an important Texas ranching family. After he inherited his parents' estate in the nineties, Max had come down and set up the picture-perfect Rancho Aria just outside of San Miguel.

Avoiding a smear of fresh chrome oxide green on my painting shirt, Maya kissed me goodbye and left. What I hadn't suggested was that she often did better interrogating guarded women than I did. I was also fairly certain that Phaedra would underestimate Maya because she was Mexican. That was always a mistake that Maya could turn to her advantage. Furthermore, Maya was used to condescending expats, and any vulnerability she might have once felt toward them was lost long ago.

At one o'clock I was cleaning my brushes. Since she was heading out to ride at Rancho Camarena after her talk with Phaedra, I didn't expect to see her for lunch. Cody called as I was washing up and said he was on the way over with two medium pizzas and did we care to be there when he arrived? He settled for my presence.

Ten minutes later we sat at the long table out in the loggia. I brought out a couple of Negra Modelos and a shaker of crushed red pepper. Orlando, our long tailed garden grackle was already pacing at the end of the table. He can smell pizza from a hundred meters away. Beak in the air, he regarded Cody with a golden eye as he lifted out a slice studded with pepperoni and jalapeños. Orlando had proven in the past that he could take the heat.

"Hope I'm not interrupting anything," Cody said, flipping a long string of cheese overhand past the end of the table, where Orlando caught it in his beak by moving only a single foot. This was a one-sided game these two had played for a long time.

"A man's got to eat sometime. I was finished with painting for the day."

He looked at me as if he knew more was coming, and there was, because we hadn't had much of a chance to talk about Rocio as a suspect. I'd been anxious to rush back and check on Maya. "Being a lefty doesn't make Rocio guilty, OK?" I continued. "Delgado's been wrong before, and far more often than we have. We don't use the same formulas that he does."

"That's why we make the big bucks." Cody dosed the slices on his half liberally with crushed pepper. I added somewhat less on mine.

"As if that would happen on this case. At least it's not a lot of travel like the last one in Chiapas, and I've got a commission for the landscape I'm working on. The guy's house is tucked into one corner of it."

"Is the house for real?"

"No, he gave me a photo and I just worked it in at his request. But what is real?"

"How about Edward Jericho? I never met him."

"No way. Rocio says reality is a condition that Edward would make a point of stepping over in the gutter, if he even noticed it in passing."

"OK. I've known a few of those, too, and you can't always blame them. Tell me some more about this Veronica thing." We had discussed this too briefly to make much sense after we left Rocio's apartment. I brought him up to date on what I'd found in the journals and from talking to Rocio.

"The most interesting idea I heard just now in what you said is that it appeared in Cuernavaca in the later sixties or early seventies," he said. "There was a lot of weird stuff going on then, culturally I mean."

"I actually haven't come across that in the journals yet. The Cuernavaca idea came from Rocio's comment about some of their conversations before she parted with Edward. But you know what I just thought of when you mentioned that? Who was also in Cuernavaca at that time? The painter Irena Karski. I find that very interesting."

"Who? That's like me mentioning an NFL quarterback to you."

"She was a Polish artist who became the icon of Art Deco painting in the twenties and thirties. When I was doing more copies than I do now, I painted two of her pictures and sold them to collectors who couldn't afford her work but didn't want to settle for a print. She had the title of baroness from her late husband, although I think she was born a commoner in Kraków. Toward the end of her life she settled in Cuernavaca and died there around 1980. Maybe her death put the relic into play then, if she had it. If I recall correctly, Irena Karski even painted a version of Veronica lifting the veil from Christ's face, maybe more than one. I'll try to find it online."

"Are you suggesting that she may have been working from life?"

I shrugged. "If you want to call that life. If I were

using it, it would only be a prop. I've got a cabinet full of them upstairs. They don't come to life unless somebody puts them on or you build them into a still life."

We worked on our pizza and stared out into the garden for a while. The banana tree was struggling with the chill again, as it always did this time of year. It would've preferred to be planted in Tabasco.

"So what's your take on Rocio Valdez?" He bit off the point of a large segment crowded with pepperoni and jalapeños. His tone suggested this was not a special question, which is how I knew that it was.

"I do like her. I appreciate the fact that she's a poet and a strong woman. Her insights can help us. She's also got more and closer recent history with Edward than anyone we know of. That counts for a lot. We can't even find anyone else to talk to here."

"I can see that, but can we dismiss her as a suspect when we don't have any others? Do you think you might be giving her a pass? Because she seems to like you too."

"I don't mind it that she likes me. It supports the idea of her possessing a strong intelligence and good taste. She bought my Raphael *tondo* at the auction, didn't she? How often in the past have tasteless dunderheads been of any use to us?"

"They're usually of use only to the other side."

"My point exactly."

CHAPTER TEN
MAYA SANCHEZ
MEANWHILE, BACK AT THE RANCH

Approaching el Rancho Aria on the Dolores Hidalgo road, Maya felt out of uniform without her half-chaps, breeches, and boots. The word *civilian* crossed her mind, but she was quick to substitute the word *investigator.* She planned to change when she arrived later at Rancho Camarena, since to wear her riding gear for the interview at Aria would only remind Phaedra Montgomery that she no longer boarded Martina there.

When Maya phoned ahead at eleven that morning the call was picked up by Phaedra's personal assistant, Gina, who informed her that she now handled the social calendar for Mrs. Montgomery-Kingman. That was a surprise.

On her arrival Maya discovered that the earlier gatekeeper, Carlos, who knew her by sight, had been replaced, so she had to surrender her driver's license to gain admittance only after her name was found on the day's visitor schedule. He gave her a small blue plastic pyramid with a number on all four sides to put on her dash. She would now be known as visitor number seven. It then occurred to her that Phaedra might have purged the staff after Max's death, which further suggested that cementing their loyalty might be an ongoing struggle for the recent widow.

Maya parked in the upper area, a level compound with a gravel surface surrounded by a row of sentry cactus that screened the guests' cars from the house. The immaculate grounds beyond, all grass, ivy, red tile roofs, pea-gravel paths, and hand-cut stone walls, worthy of a spread in *Town and Country*, were washed and polished by the sun and the clear and cool midday air.

Gina met her at the door, a woman with a neutral demeanor. Her thin dark hair had been pulled into an efficient bun, and she offered no particular charm or good looks to grace her welcome. In the glare of Phaedra's sun, Maya observed, Gina would always find herself in deep shadow. Everybody would know who they should be looking at. Her command of English suggested she was an American, but her looks were Hispanic.

Inside the house, Maya walked with her through the great room. There were the six large Art Deco-period Leyendecker paintings that illustrated the Kingman lifestyle of three generations back, at a time when the family yacht was moored and the horses corralled in

Connecticut, probably within sight of each other. Each picture was now tastefully spotlighted, even at midday. The subtle highlights on the Duesenberg's hood and fenders still glowed with the warmth of ownership. The man standing next to it held in his raised gloved hand the reins of what Maya recognized as a Dutch Warmblood, a breed that had long provided established winners in dressage, jumping, and eventing.

The old Kingman family furniture from Texas, if now overly well seasoned, was unchanged as if it were a monument to a treasured tradition, now slightly but still fashionably passé, an era of informal elegance and character. Maya couldn't help wonder what that had all come to now in Phaedra's hands. Nothing ever lasts but the art, she said to herself, putting her speculations aside. That was what Paul would've said, had he come along with her. Even without him she knew it was true. Just as she had always provided him with an experienced eye for the nuance of Mexican culture, he had always been her practiced eye for art.

When Phaedra Montgomery received Maya on the rear terrace, Gina retired out of view, if not out of earshot or command. The setting was covered to the weather with yellow canvas, but open on three sides to the mild breeze winding down from the dry distant hills.

The large circular limestone table at the center was unchanged. This was the spot where Max Kingman had chosen to hold court from his wheelchair at the annual boarders' welcoming party six months earlier, an event that had been punctuated by a murder during the cocktail course. His widow now reigned in his place.

Phaedra Montgomery, the noted actress somewhat past her prime, did not rise to greet her, but Maya recalled her as a woman about five foot ten with a projecting bosom that had benefited from careful structural enhancement at key points. The aggressiveness of her corsets may also have propelled much of her body mass upward into this carefully pruned and fortified enclosure, although balance might have offered a problem after a few drinks. Her hair, a silvery bronze in color, seemed to have already been the object of serious effort that morning from a staff member, possibly a talented amateur sculptor. Phaedra now appeared to be stabilized at a point in her early fifties, and, Maya felt, if money could buy permanence, she was not likely to visibly grow much older.

"Won't you sit down, please," the diva said to Maya. "And have we met before? Please refresh my mind. I'm sure you understand that I meet so many people here."

Only about four times have we met, Maya thought, including a one on one interview that lasted half an hour at this same table five months ago. Still, she was pleased to be granted an anonymously fresh start. It wouldn't have been helpful to be loaded with the baggage of that previous case now.

"Only briefly," she said. "It was at a social event here at the ranch where there were many other guests. But I want to first tell you how sad I was to hear about Mr. Kingman's passing."

"Ah, yes, well! Thank you. It's been nearly three months now. It was a terrible shock even to the staff, and, so much more, such a deep disruption here, where our ongoing training mission is so critical. But things are settling down again now as we pass Max's legacy on to others. Rancho Aria is all about the future now."

"I'm sure." From down the slope at the paddock Maya could hear a pair of horses calling to each other, their voices borne southward toward the house on the wind.

"Can I offer you some coffee or tea? It's still quite early in the day for me."

"Coffee, please." By Maya's watch it was 11:50.

Phaedra made a subtle motion with her left hand and a moment later the houseboy appeared with a tray of coffee and tea, cream and sugar, and several kinds of pastry with untouched pots of butter and jam. Watching her pour, Maya reflected that it was fortunate the terrace was covered, since otherwise the sun-induced glare from the diamond on Phaedra's left hand might have caused some damage to her unprotected corneas. Unthinkingly, she had left her sunglasses in the van. Phaedra waited to speak again until the server had departed after pouring.

"I understand you have some questions about our former connection with that painter fellow, Edward Jericho." Her tone suggested that this occupation might lack a few degrees of respectability in some circles. From living with Paul, Maya already knew this was true. To her, it was this same divergence from mainstream values that gave it some excitement.

"Yes. His body was discovered within the past few days, buried in the garden of the house he rented in town."

"So Gina informed me after you called. I'm sure that was most unfortunate. For myself, of course, given my background, I feel that murder is so dreadfully vulgar, but it does still tend to explain why Edward was so lax in paying his board bills. I always prefer to think there are better ways to settle disputes among civilized people of a certain class. Don't you agree, ah..?" Phaedra's index finger traced an uncertain but vaguely seismic line over the table.

"Maya Sanchez." Her grin carefully masked her perfect teeth.

"Yes, thank you." Phaedra raised her teacup an inch in tribute to this reminder and then took a thoughtful sip.

"Of course," Maya said, staring into her cup, "I

was named Maria at birth." At least the strong coffee was excellent, if the company was somewhat weaker. "What I wanted to ask you was whether in the months before Edward stopped paying his board you had noticed anything that might have been threatening to him. Perhaps you saw something change in his manner."

Phaedra stared back at her for a long moment, her cup poised in the air. "Well, that, of course, would be an issue somewhat beyond my normal rounds. We all have our natural boundaries here in the great house, and they tend to exclude those aspects of the estate that carry any element of trade, if you know what I'm saying."

"Business, you mean," said Maya.

"Well, yes, as you might call it here." She stole a subtle glance at her watch, but not so subtle that Maya missed it.

"So you didn't ever deal with Edward Jericho personally when he was boarding here? Did you even know him?"

Phaedra returned an offhand shrug. "Oh, I believe I must have met him at one or another of our social things. Of course, there are so many people here then, it's hard to keep track of them all in a crowd like that, try as I might."

"So you don't specifically recall him?" Maya was now thinking of herself as only another filmy face in that crowd.

"Right, or any of the other *customers*, really. The trade parts of the estate were always Max's job, the dear old thing. I do so miss him now. But on this topic, I think you should more properly be speaking with Rodrigo, down at the livestock pens. He's the trainer now. I do wish Gina had told me what this was about in more detail. We could've saved some time for both of us. I think you can find your own way down there?"

With a shallow smile of early dismissal, Phaedra rose to say goodbye, dropping her linen napkin next to her teacup.

Setting her half full cup aside, Maya actually welcomed this. She recalled Rodrigo well from her own months of boarding at Rancho Aria, which had already been Martina's home for a while when Maya bought her. Rodrigo displayed an intermittent drinking problem around holidays, but his insightful and personal relationship with the horses was always a major asset to the ranch.

Moving down the slope three minutes later she saw him finishing the bathing of Camembert, one of the spirited offspring of Madrigal, the dressage champion of Rancho Aria. When she came closer she saw that Rodrigo's three missing front teeth had been replaced. He was also dressed a bit better than before when he was only a groom.

"Good morning, Señorita Sanchez. Are you

coming back to board? We have kept a space or two wait-ing for Martina." As she glanced around it appeared to Maya that only about half of the two dozen stalls were in use.

"No, but thank you. She's happily settled in now among her new friends, but I know she misses your kind touch. Is Señor Braganza still working here?" She looked toward the tack room. He was the trainer hired to replace the murdered Raul in the earlier case.

Rodrigo paused and wiped his hands on his jeans. His frayed straw hat still gave him the *campesino* look, and his denim jacket was well seasoned. "The *señor* trainer left soon after the death of Señor Kingman. I am happy to be his substitute now, unless the *señora* finds a new one. I trust that God will prevent this."

Keep them off balance, Maya thought. It's become all about loyalty to the new management since Phaedra took over. "How is Diego doing now?" This was Edward's Azteca.

"Oh, Diego was sold since long ago, Señorita Sanchez, because the board was not paid. Do you know this? (Of course she did.) Even the tack for him was sold too, to a private rider we do not know before. But one day he comes with a receipt from the Señora Kingman and took it away. Well, some of it he took away."

This was the question Maya had wanted to ask, but no longer needed to. "So this man knew what he wanted and it was not everything. Was he an American?"

"He was not a Mexican but not an American, either. I don't know from where he comes, although his skin was a bit darker than the American riders here. He possessed little Spanish." Rodrigo laughed uneasily, as he often did when he was faced with gringo clients of higher status but much lower equestrian knowledge or skills than he had. This happened nearly every day at the rancho.

When Maya did not respond he went on, as if he felt prodded just a bit. "Well, he seemed to know what he wanted." To say much more was to infringe on the turf of people not of his class. "With him he took away the dressage saddle, even though when I asked him, he said he did not yet have a horse. You would think he would buy it for a particular horse, yes? But no, so I do not ask more. The three bridles, the four fly masks, the two sets of polo wraps, the saddle pads, and the halters and all the rest. He left everything but the saddle behind."

Nodding to keep this list going, Maya saw immediately what it meant. The tack outside of the saddle was costly too. The purchaser must have been a person who didn't ride. So what were his reasons for buying the saddle if the other necessities of riding had been abandoned?

"Did he tell you his name?" Maya doubted she could ever get this from Phaedra, if she had even taken note of it.

"No. I do not ask him. It might have been on the receipt, but he kept it."

"So we have no way to know who he was?"

"I am sorry, but no. Although he had one odd thing about him, I can tell you this now. I saw when he bends over to pick up the saddle, he has a small tattoo on the back of his neck."

"Yes?" Maya was thinking it would be a woman's name inside a heart.

"It was of an eye with a small pupil, and two lines coming lower from it, one straight down, like this, and the other curved backward with a hook at the bottom."

In the dust on the tool bench he drew a quick sketch.

Maya was not sure why a chill would be moving down her spine at this image. "Thank you, Rodrigo, I am so happy to have talked with you today. I will give your greetings to Martina!"

"*Gracias, Señorita!*"

Maya drove back home in a pensive frame of mind. The graphic symbol Rodrigo had drawn was the Eye of Horus. She had often seen it used in jewelry with a New Age theme, but she also knew it was Egyptian in its origin, and dating to the time of the pharaohs. Given what Paul had told her about Edward's taste for the ancient world, she was not altogether surprised, even if this symbol possessed far earlier roots than anything in Christianity. Was it possible the Veronica did too?

A tougher question was what significance, if any, it might have today. Suppose the buyer of the saddle had dozens of other tattoos showing trendy logos, but the Eye of Horus on his neck was the only one visible outside of his clothes.

CHAPTER ELEVEN

May 18

After an archival search that was truly serpentine, I finally located what is close to a complete transcript of the Chet Scribner interview with Baroness Irena Karski in Cuernavaca. When published in August of 1975 in Art Horizons Today, it had been badly cut (for my purposes, anyway). But the Internet, as always, came through. It's a shame she was so skittish, but she was already in her late 70s then. I can almost hear her thick Polish accent, but here's the relevant part:

Karski: "But when you ask that, what are you thinking of to be an artifact, you of the magazine media? Each of my works is an artifact. That of any great painter must be. What is of the first importance is that this be recognized in the artist's own time."

Scribner: "Well that's one of the reasons I'm

here to speak with you tonight."

Karski: "Ha! But you are very much late with this now. I would've talked to you with more enthusiasm in 1926. Today everyone knows me, so I don't need you. Find someone new and fresh, be a discoverer of original talent if you wish to be of service to the world of art. Here you are following an old trail, and one that will soon grow cold."

Scribner: "But that relates to what I wanted to ask you next. There is a rumor that you have an ancient artifact in your possession."

Karski: "And what would that be?"

Scribner: "Well, you used it in several of your paintings."

Karski: "I don't want to talk about this. I have had some trouble already. Shut this down. Do not use this part. I am pulling this thing off my collar now..."

I could almost hear the Baroness Karski's voice rising in irate passion as she fumbled with the microphone clip. She clearly felt invaded. This passage in Edward's journal was so far from the medieval quotes, the pious ramblings of the Dark Ages, the insider comments about the Crusades as if they were still tucked back in living memory, I felt like it was a breakthrough. This interview was from only forty-some years ago. What had Edward thought when he found it? Was it a door opening onto the artifact itself? But apparently there was no more on that subject when the interview resumed, because he included nothing else from it in the transcript. It made me wonder whether she had added something off the record that the mike had missed.

Throughout this process I'd been aware that I had still avoided rushing to the back of one of these volumes to see how it ended. Not that I thought it ever did. I surely didn't expect that the final page would conclude with a half finished sentence, "and then he came running up behind me with a knife in his left hand…"

Later Maya came into the studio and stood in the blazing light from the south windows. This time of year I always drew the drapes when I was painting, but I had finished. It was mid afternoon and she still wore her half chaps, small blunt spurs, and breeches. It was her sports look; trim, tight, and toned.

"You look like you had an interesting time today," I said, glancing at the journal I had set aside, bookmarked. "Did Phaedra treat you well?"

"Not exactly, but I think I still found out something at Aria when I was down in the 'livestock pens,' as she called the paddock. You can tell me what you think. Have you ever heard of the Eye of Horus?"

"Sure. You see it on pendants a lot. It came into fashion in the late sixties along with the ankh and a number of other pseudo-mystical things, although they surely would've had some mystical meaning in their time."

"Would you ever wear it as a tattoo?"

"Me?" I looked up at her. "I wouldn't wear anything as a tattoo. Did you notice it on Phaedra? I would've thought her style was more classic than that. I can imagine the sneer on her face at the idea."

Maya went on to tell me about her meeting with Rodrigo. "What do you think it means?"

"I don't know," I said. "Maybe nothing. If you were walking down the street and you saw someone with that tattoo on the back of his neck would you give it any real significance?"

"Probably not. Not everything you see is a clue, even though it may mean something. But when Rodrigo said this guy took only the saddle, and that happening after all the chair seats that were slashed in two break-ins? Well, what do you think?"

"I think he's an agent of the upholstery industry drumming up business. Does that saddle come apart?"

"Of course, it's adjustable to fit the horse's back."

"Was he an American?"

"No, but not Mexican either. That's another thing. This man was a gringo with somewhat darker skin, Rodrigo said. He couldn't offer more than that. You know, he's not educated."

"But you think Rodrigo was replacing that other trainer who came from the north? Braganza, I think his name was?"

"Yes, and again, it may be only because of his loyalty to Phaedra. Rodrigo said his job was temporary, which is a way she can hold it over his head to keep him in line. He was always a fine groom, but he'll never be a trainer. It's paying off for him, since he now has new teeth for those missing three across the top where he was kicked by Madrigal."

"This will be the end of Rancho Aria."

"Of course, as a serious training ranch, but when was it ever that? It will still always *look* like the best; you can count on that, just as Phaedra will always look good. It'll draw the local gringos like it eternally has, but appearance is mainly what that appeal rests on. That won't change. It's Connecticut with salsa dancing. It's Equestria South."

We both considered this for a moment. "You look good without all that help," I said. "It comes from inside."

"So do you. You don't even have any paint on your skin today." She gave me her special grin.

"I cleaned up early, thinking of you." That wasn't true, but it was always a great pick up line. I set the journal volume aside.

Forty minutes later I pulled my jeans back on, and searching for my shirt, walked past the line of half chaps, breeches, spurs, and underwear that led back to the studio. I couldn't find both of my shoes, but the sun coming through the south windows had heated the floor, so it wasn't critical at that moment. Maya had been her affectionately playful self in bed, and we'd lingered for a while afterward. I think we were both happy to be thinking about something more basic and appealing than the Jericho case. It gave both of us the feeling of clinging to something filmy and insubstantial. Maybe that was only because Edward had been gone so long.

As I buttoned my shirt and sat down on the same wicker chair, I stared again at the Mazilu painting on the wall. I had positioned it to catch my eye during pensive moments like this.

I was also thinking in sharp contrast how the Baroness Karski interview segment had been so unsatisfying. Chet Scribner could've been talking about any historic relic, although he seemed to refer to her Veronica painting. What else could've spooked her like that? She hadn't come on at all like a vulnerable old lady, although she was close to eighty then. She was only frightened. "I have had some trouble already," she'd said, as if she expected more. To me that suggested that the trouble, whatever it was, had been unsuccessful in achieving its goal. It had only made her more cautious. She was afraid someone was coming back.

I moved to the laptop for a while, searching for the Baroness and her biography. I already knew her paintings well. She had lived in an old mansion in a fashionable part of Cuernavaca. Of course she had some money from her own painting career, if she had hung onto it, and whatever had come from her late husband, Baron Karski. Her companion in México had been a much younger man reputed to be gay. He probably worshipped her, and he was also her heir.

Two paragraphs further down in the article was a segment on her passing. In August of 1980 she had been found in her bedroom comatose from a blow to the head, and expired in the hospital the following day without regaining consciousness. It was assumed to be a home invasion, and no one was ever arrested in her death. If anything was thought to be missing from the premises, it was not mentioned. After her passing, her companion dutifully scattered her ashes via helicopter into the crater of Mount Popocatepetl, the great active volcano between Mexico City and Puebla. She was eighty-one years old. But nothing further in these entries helped me with the Veronica. I held the only recent primary source in my own hands, if Edward's journals were even worthy of being called that.

As I lifted the other journal volume from the table it slipped from my hand, falling face down and open onto the tile floor. As it fell, a single sheet flew out and settled beneath my wicker chair. I dragged it out with my sock clad toe. It was a piece of old laid paper, buff colored, the ribs clearly visible in that afternoon light. It was not a page ripped from the journal—the paper was not a match. There, in a writing style much different from that of Edward's hand, I saw this undated notation:

Like a wight,
Who haply from Croatia wends to see
Our Veronica, O and, the while 'tis shown,
Hangs over it with never-sated gaze,
And, all that he hath heard revolving, saith
Unto himself in thought: "And didst Thou look
E'en thus, O Jesus, my true Lord and God?
And was this semblance Thine?" So gazed I then
Adoring...

    —Dante, Canto XXXI, The Divine
       Comedy, circa 1310

Here, uniquely, was a source of impeccable provenance! Even so, I also quickly verified the quote online.

How handy it would've been if Dante had also mentioned the location of the Veronica at that time, or given us the name of the Croatian traveler to pursue in the archives. In terms of its whereabouts today, it wouldn't have been that helpful, but as another link in the chain, priceless, given the credibility of the source. Dante must have found the object more than at least plausible to include it, since he certainly implies it was the goal of a pilgrimage.

With its watery brown fountain pen ink and loopy but controlled style, the texture of this document between my fingers felt old and European. I had the sudden thought it might have come from the hand of Baroness Irena Karski, but that would've been a long shot indeed. Like other key characters in this story, there was no way to ask her. We'd never done an investigation where some of the information sources were more than a thousand years old. If the Agency ever reached the point of writing up a case record for this romp, I might be tempted to call it *Absent Witnesses*.

CHAPTER TWELVE

It was the following morning, and after a night interrupted by my fragmentary musings about the Veronica, Maya had gone to the ranch to ride after breakfast. I was at the easel painting highlights on my landscape. I was close to finishing that picture, a phase where I get up and study the canvas from three steps back every ten minutes or so to see what's missing, or what needs a gentle boost. Sometimes I turn it upside down, a perspective that's quick to reveal flaws in the composition. At other times I turn it against the wall and walk away to think about something else. In this case, my mind wandered back to the excerpt from *The Divine Comedy*.

My dictionary defined *wight* as a sentient being, and offered not much more, aside from furnishing a number of references in the works of Chaucer, a near contemporary of Dante.

It also traced its use in writing as recent as that of Tolkien in *The Lord of the Rings*. I knew he was nearly a contemporary of Irena Karski. I also could see these were idle and unproductive thoughts. Like the Veronica itself, this case was a ghostly fabric made from an uncertain substance; it seemed like there was nothing solid to reach out to. The only real artifacts we had were those we'd won in the auction.

Thinking about this, once again my eye paused on the Mazilu portrait. I took it down to examine the brushwork, holding it edge on to the light. The man had a delicate and precise hand. The paint was applied in thin, exact strokes that in their fluid smoothness did not stand up at all from the surface at the edges. The texture of the linen canvas was delicate and nearly invisible. It was so smooth that the primer may have been sanded with a superfine grit. This was not at all my style of painting, but it exhibited a flowing mastery I had to admire, even that close. Like any painter, when looking at the work of another, I can often see how it would have appeared if it had sprung from my own brush.

The gilt frame had also come from the hand of a skillful craftsman–framing is an art in itself–with a carved and subtly raised foliage motif at the corners where the members met in a miter. Turning it to look at the back, I expected to find the label of a gallery, possibly in Paris, where Georges Mazilu used to live. Instead, the usual brown paper dust cover, carefully glued down all around the stretchers, was lacking any notation. I had been hoping a European label might give me some clue about Edward's travels. This fruitless search only made me realize how little I had to go on, as always.

I was finished for the day, although I'd only been working for an hour and a half. You can only go along as far as it works. The last effort on a painting (like many other things) is often the hardest because it involves deciding when to stop, always from instinct more than formula. I cleaned my brushes and washed up before I sat down again in the wicker chair. Randomly opening the second journal volume—I didn't see the first one nearby—somewhere past the middle, I came across this:

December 4

And then there was Raynaud de Chatillon. Not the familiar and sinister figure of the Second Crusade, of course, but a renegade buccaneer nonetheless who had borrowed this noble name for his own purposes. I can always see them coming. At first I thought he hoped to reach the Veronica through me, but his approach came through Rocio. By that time I had felt her loyalty weakening for some time. I don't understand why, when I was closer than ever before to my triumph. I was more powerful than I had been since she joined me. Why did my progress somehow threaten her? There was never any jealousy between us before. She had her own place in our relationship and I had mine.

I almost cringed at reading this, since I had been avoiding those notes that directly concerned Rocio, but this one was so closely linked to the Veronica that I couldn't ignore it. Perhaps Raynaud's "approach" to her was so minor that she hardly noticed, or had even misinterpreted it. A lot of men might have eyed her hopefully and he may not have stood out among them. Or perhaps it had been far more than that and she'd chosen to withhold that encounter from me. And why not? After all, it was no business of mine, and she had never asked me to involve myself in Edward's death. Still, I felt compelled to bring it up to her if I could find the right moment. I didn't think I could just show up at her apartment on Calle San Francisco and lay it out for her. It required a less direct approach.

The truth was that the Paul Zacher Agency had virtually no standing in this investigation. As next of kin, Dillon Gericault had not asked us to take an interest, and even Diego Delgado had bluntly inquired whether anyone had hired us. I was not usually shy about asking questions, but this situation had given me no moral courage or any real sense of a mission whatever. The word *pushy* now often came to mind.

Over the next several days I ruminated about this without coming up with a solution. I roughed in a new landscape with mining ruins in a half-distracted way, based on some photos I had taken in Pozos, a nearby semi-ghost town, two years earlier. Finally an invitation to the Edward Jericho memorial framed in an email message hit my computer screen, and it quickly set the game in motion once again.

CHAPTER THIRTEEN

Whoever had planned Edward's memorial service had been knowledgeable enough about the January climate to schedule it for the mid afternoon. Nine in the morning in that frigid month would've had a chilling effect beyond what was appropriate even for an event like that. It was the end of the month and we were waiting without success for the warmer weather to begin. Maya had put on layers of clothing in different sequences and was agonizing about her wardrobe up until the moment we walked out the door at 2:15.

The expat section of the Panteón is part of a more recent annex that runs along the far left corner. An iron gate links it with the larger and older Mexican burial ground. The graves in this subdivision, mostly American and Canadian, are more somber and less crowded together. It's a calmer style of death with a slow, contemplative feeling. The residents have time to kick back and review their lives in a more tranquil setting, without being interrupted by music and fireworks. In the much larger Mexican section, individual style is still highly sought after, and the graves, mostly above ground and jostling each other shoulder-to-shoulder like the houses in town, continue to display a creative and improvisational bravura that may not have been available to many of the inhabitants during life.

The gathered memorial assembly was not large, perhaps thirty-five or forty people at most. Edward Jericho had been a private person, and judging from the host who checked off our names at the gate, admission to the service must have been by invitation only. I remembered that Dillon had used Rocio Valdez to help him assemble the list, which was why the entire Zacher Agency was included. I had already picked out Edward's twin at the front, wearing a crisp tropical suit that may have been too optimistic for the weather. At 6400 feet here, the tropics are nowhere in view from San Miguel, although April and May can make you sweat. Maya had settled on a pair of dark gray wool slacks with a hint of a flair at the ankle, and a navy V-neck sweater with a pale gray cotton turtleneck under it. Cody looked a bit shoehorned into a black double-breasted suit I had never seen him wear before. I could imagine it may have seen some prior use in his detective days for burying coworkers, but not much since. I wore freshly pressed khaki slacks and a blazer I hadn't used in years. I had to dust the shoulders off when

I took it out of my armoire.

When he turned to scan the crowd I saw that Dillon Gericault bore an ordinary fraternal resemblance to Edward, but I wouldn't have guessed they were twins. If anything, he looked somewhat older and less determined, with a few streaks of gray in his dark hair. I saw a slight tentativeness in his gestures and a mild vagueness in his bearing. Perhaps he was not fully comfortable finding himself in México. I wondered whether he also felt the uneasiness that the death of a twin must bring, as if he'd been cut loose from a mooring that had secured him his whole life, although an anchor to Edward would've been sunk in shifting sands. I had no idea how close Dillon had been with his brother in later years, but there was always that undeniable link of nearly simultaneous birth. I'm sure they had always known which one was older and taunted each other with it.

A man I didn't recognize offered the eulogy. He wore a fuchsia ecclesiastical shirt, subtly pleated in front, with a vaguely clerical collar under a black jacket. When he turned to face the mourners his expression was welcoming if not upbeat. Many in that small crowd were people we knew. At least three of them besides me were also painters, but there was not much exchange among us as we waited to begin.

Grave markers of a similar design occupied most of this quiet shady lawn; limestone tablets, wider than they were tall, with a shallow arched top. I recognized more than a few names. This was a variety of stone that would never hold its shape against the wind, rain, and weather as well as granite and many other varieties. Within a couple of generations the letters would begin to grow soft and blurred along the edges. It was as if the expat dead here did not insist on being remembered eternally. By the time the lettering was indistinct beyond recognition no one would be alive who could recall who they'd been anyway. The overall sense was that of peaceful civility, and murder as a cause of death was not a good fit there.

At a signal from the celebrant, we all moved closer on a neatly raked gravel path and spread out along several rows. Along the boundary behind him stretched a wall of square niches framed in concrete four tiers high, and a bronze urn had been placed in one at eye level near the center of the series. After the service the opening would be covered and the facing inscribed. I wondered if Edward had specified his epitaph too. It would've been like him to be particular about that. In the spirit of his paintings, I could also imagine a weeping Victorian angel bent over his niche, although these narrow spaces didn't provide enough space for such displays.

In calm and reassuring tones the pastor talked about the connection between art and life for eight or ten minutes. About how the creative impulse provides a way to make sense of life that people who are not painters or writers do not usually possess. I thought some of it was on the mark, as if the man had really known Edward and discussed some of these ideas with him. I know he had enjoyed theorizing about his painting and how copying the work of great masters from the past gave meaning to his life. For me, the idea that a creative career was a way to relate to an often hostile and unconnected world held a lot of wisdom. Art is a system and an interconnected reality that has a coherence that, in its randomness, the outside reality lacks. The speaker made no mention of God or eternity, but he did say that great art lasted longer than any of us, a reassuring thought of minor league perpetuity I've often had as well.

As it continued I felt Edward might have enjoyed this service. It offered an emphasis on personal development and the pursuit of focused individual dreams, but nothing in it suggested Edward's passing was anything but natural. During this I also watched Rocio for some time. She was wearing a black pantsuit and she had a prominent place in the front row. I couldn't see her face, but from her lack of movement and her unwavering upright posture she seemed composed, if not especially connected to Dillon. She didn't turn toward him or the speaker much and was possibly lost in her own thoughts, as many of us also were.

Dillon and a much shorter woman I didn't

recognize faced the group in turn to make brief tributes to Edward. As if they had never been close, Dillon's were vague and not very insightful, but I got the sense from her remarks that she may have narrowly failed to marry Edward in their youth, although he had never mentioned any near misses in my presence. There was no reason why he would. Rocio did not speak.

At the end the officiant advised us to go in peace. There were no prayers aside from a final *Amen*.

If after Edward's long absence the memorial was not an emotionally charged occasion, it was still a genteel closure to a creative life cut short. I was modestly moved by it, imagining a calm and clear-headed ceremony like this for myself. Maya, of course, would be convulsed with grief at my passing, leaning on Cody's arm throughout for support, even to stay upright. Dependable friend that he was, he would be sure to take exquisite care in consoling her. Then, within seconds after the mourning period expired, he would be dating her. What are friends for?

Maya's face held a neutral and relaxed look as she listened. She'd known Edward even less than I had. Because she and I had talked on many occasions about painting technique (usually mine), I knew she had a more limited appreciation of what Edward had done than I did.

If I could've edited the text of Edward's service beforehand, I would've inserted a section in this eulogy about his lengthy pursuit of the Veronica, and how some people can discover meaning in unlikely objects. I would've suggested that the chase is often more important than the outcome, but clearly the good reverend had known nothing about Edward's quest. I couldn't imagine that Dillon had either or he would've informed him of it. It could have added an agreeable footnote to the larger picture and humanized a service that seemed slightly abstract because Edward had already been gone so long. This made me make a note to rethink the question of whether to send Dillon his brother's journals when this case was finished.

As silence fell over the gathering, many of the mourners filed up and placed a single bloom in the niche. Not anticipating this finish, and arriving at the last minute, we hadn't thought to bring any flowers, although we could've bought them at the gate coming in, so we faded back. People gave each other a firm handshake and an occasional kiss on the cheek. When the front row was reduced to only Rocio, who hadn't moved other than to acknowledge condolences from six or eight people and then bid them goodbye, I waved Maya and Cody away.

"I want to talk to Rocio for a minute or two," I whispered. "I'll meet you at the car in just a bit, but if I don't show up within a reasonable time, then I'll walk home. Don't wait too long for me and don't worry. There's something I have to ask her about that came up in the journals."

Nodding in silence, Maya took Cody's arm and they left at the same measured pace as the others, but trailing the group.

It was a short interval after the expat section had emptied before Rocio slowly turned. I was studying the names on the markers as I waited and I was sure she expected to find herself alone, in sole command of that peaceful terrain. When I saw the surprise in her face I almost thought she was going to say she didn't want to talk to me. Instead she gave me a weary, but not unwelcoming smile. I saw in her features no strong element of grief; in fact, she looked as if she had learned something within the last half hour, perhaps more about herself and her reactions than about her late partner.

"I'm very tired," she said. "Don't expect a lot from me after this, but thank you for coming. I can feel your support."

"I wanted to have just a few words with you about an old friend."

"So you must have been a close friend of Edward's, even more than I thought." She came forward and clutched my hand. Hers was slightly cooler than mine.

"Not that close. Now, after seeing this, I wonder if I even knew him as well as I imagined. Of course, what he was doing in his painting told me, or anyone else that could see it, a great deal about him, more than what he actually said to me when we met. Still, I'm going to need your help in understanding him in other ways." I said this to open a door for a more probing conversation with her. I wasn't sure she wanted to have one.

Rocio turned and gently offered me her arm as we walked out through the iron gates into the main cemetery. All the other mourners had gone on ahead of us, none lingering in the brighter and far more picturesque Mexican section. It carried an altogether different message. The silence was now complete, since the three groundskeepers were working on the far side by the north wall, and there were no other visitors in sight. We strolled along the rows of extravagant, highly personal expressions of mourning. They ranged from prayer to protest to penance. In comparison the expat grave markers had been mute and nearly anonymous, almost defeated in their unprotesting sameness. It seemed as if they no longer spoke for any individual, but only for death itself as a general condition, a state of mind all held in common. In every case the markers felt more final. In that part of the compound, death resembled frustration more than release.

Still, the deceased Mexicans now around us found no reason to remain silent about their fate—and fate is how many of them would've regarded it. Here was triumphant eternity trumpeting over death. The littered flowers had soon wilted and dried, and burned out votive candles waited by the hundreds near the broken concrete sculptures. The cracked sepulchers were launched into the hereafter like ghost ships about to sink ten feet off the end of the pier. The feathery tips of angels' wings were crushed in the gravel beneath our feet.

While the message was eternity, the condition was instant deterioration, a contradiction perfectly tuned for México. Truth often has an irreconcilable dualism here that we don't always find elsewhere. No attempt is made to resolve opposites. In happy coexistence they can even party together. At another moment I might have considered his further, but Rocio pulled me back to the present. With her tug on my arm we came to a stop.

"Maybe this is a good time and place for what you want to say to me, Paul." She didn't look at my face. We stood near a series of four side-by-side tombs of the *familia* Bustamante, closer than they'd probably been in life. Was it the same auction family? When I said nothing we moved along, reached the top of the row and round-ed into the next, where a devil wrestled with an angel on the cover of the first burial. I couldn't determine who was winning. The conflict may have been more the point than the outcome. Somehow this reminded me of Edward. In the memorial service the word peace had never come up in regard to him, only to the mourners. His end had certainly left none of us in peace.

"This is as good a time and place as any, but I don't want to disturb you in your grief." I hadn't meant to start with that, but I suddenly wasn't sure what Rocio was feeling and I wanted to reach out to her that much.

"For me, today I think it was less about grief than about closure. You know how long it's been. I want the Edward Jericho I used to know to have some peace now, as I do for myself."

"And did the service work that way for you?"

"Yes, I think it did. Of course, I had closure of one kind before, when we broke up. While I didn't believe we would ever get back together, I never thought it was as final as what we saw this afternoon. It's painful to think that Edward's not still out there, somewhere, on onc of his searches."

"I'm sure." Even staring into her face this closely now I saw no trace of tears in her eyes. I thought again of Delgado's idea that she might have killed Edward and how wrong that had to be.

We walked on to the end of the row and turned again. She had made no attempt to continue toward the gate, which would've ended the conversation. I took this to mean she was now invested in it.

"You're a searcher too, aren't you, Paul? What are you looking for today?" Rocio stopped to face me, leaning against a white painted burial that crudely depicted Christ leaping off the cross, his black hair wild and his arms extended in ecstasy and triumph. In contrast, her arms were now folded closely against her chest. There was no triumph to be found for her in any part of this day. I wondered whether the white paint would mark her black slacks. It sometimes has a chalky texture, and she still looked immaculate and composed, even in her expression.

"I can answer that. First, I wanted to let you know that I have found Edward's journals, the last two volumes anyway. They were in that box of his art books I bought at the auction. I only discovered that after you and I spoke that first time. I hadn't even gone through all those books yet."

She regarded me soberly, as if this news was not encouraging. If she was wondering why the journals hadn't come up when Cody and I came to her rescue on the night of the break in, she said nothing. Certainly I hadn't thought of them in those circumstances, and even if I had I hadn't been ready to tell her about my discovery yet.

"So that must make for very interesting reading," she said evenly with a heavy trace of irony. I now began to feel I had given her bad news. "You've probably learned a lot of things that other people can only speculate about. Consider me part of that eager group. You must be inside Edward's head now in ways I could never be when I was with him." Her eyes locked on mine. I felt I had suddenly become a coconspirator in their ex-pired conflict. "I wonder what you've discovered about me in those pages? For example, was I a good lover in bed?" Her eyebrows lifted to underline the question. I detected a trace of steel in her tone, and after a moment she looked away down the row, as if recalling not a single event, but a long series of them. "That was something he never shared with me. Now, I think I'd like to know. Perhaps you and I telling some further truths about Edward could also be part of this memorial service." Here she looked around. "Although the others may not care to hear it, but now we're alone."

I shifted my weight slightly to allow this barrage to pass harmlessly over my right shoulder. "Perhaps you think I'm now the holder of those keys, but as I've gone through these pages I've tried to avoid the more personal entries in order to focus on the Veronica. You can see why I might do that."

She smiled wryly. "Of course, of course. I know that. You are a person with a certain moral standard. You wished to respect my privacy. But I can also imagine that hasn't worked entirely, has it?"

"No, not entirely. I really wish it had." I could hear the frustration in my voice. We were silent for a while as I waited for her to speculate on what else I had found, but she didn't. "Complicating this is that I always encounter the filter of Edward's own point of view on

153

whatever he mentions, not only you, Rocio. Most of it is really focused on the Veronica, but he's never an objective source on his own life."

"I'm sure he isn't, other than to himself, and perhaps not even then. That was one of our problems toward the end. Please go on." She was staring at the red brick paved path at her feet.

Here was the crux. "Well, at one point the Veronica narrative crosses over and connects to you more directly."

Her eyebrows went up. "And? I'm sure I never saw it."

"No, and he doesn't suggest you had, but I'd like to ask you to tell me about Raynaud de Chatillon."

At this her shoulders drooped a fraction of an inch and a furrow clouded her brow. Her eyes flickered over the field of graves and found nothing to rest on. "Yes, well that would be Ray. Of course I should've seen this coming." With a twist to her lips she shook her head, but when she didn't offer any more I went on.

"I couldn't find much about him in the journals, although there might still be more. I haven't looked carefully through all of it. In what I found, Edward mainly said that Raynaud was trying to reach the Veronica through you. Does that suggest the man you call Ray thought Edward had already acquired it?" This was also a way of asking how well she knew him.

"Ray did think that at first, but I convinced him it wasn't true. Edward would never have been able to hide it from me if he had."

We started walking again. "Was that Ray's real name?"

She chuckled. "No. Nothing much was real about Ray. A few things, perhaps. He could be formidable in his own way."

"You mean in ways that he came up with, but not anyone else."

"Yes. Exactly."

I began to wonder whether Rocio Valdez tended to mainly attract men who held only a tenuous engagement with the real world. Was she a fantasy in herself? Or perhaps Ray's earthly connection ran deep, but the surface layers remained thin and shadowy. Still, what did that say about her? Edward had only done copies. Was his life also a copy of someone else's? Was he in the habit of assuming the identity of the painter whose work he was copying? If so, did that make him a figure larger than himself?

"What was Ray up to?"

"I suppose you could say Ray was another man on a mission, one not so different from Edward's. Or even from yours."

This looked like an implied question I was not going to answer. "Was he really French?"

She shook her head. "No, he was Lebanese. I saw his passport once when it fell out of his pocket. He had hung his pants over the back of a chair." She didn't look at me and her stride seemed to grow longer, and even if it didn't quicken much, her step was still firmer. Did I see a sudden trace of defiance in the angle she held her chin?

"I see. That would explain Edward's tone when he wrote about him. Did Ray contribute to the end of your relationship with Edward too?"

"Of course. By that time nearly everything I did contributed to it, like what time it was when I got up in the morning. Nothing was right anymore. I couldn't make soup right, or even coffee."

"But Ray was right? I'm not trying to violate your privacy, Rocio, but if Ray was part of the other side in the struggle to recover the Veronica, then I need to know more about him."

She smiled for the first time. When she spoke her tone became broader and more open. "No, Ray wasn't right either, at least not for me. Not that I understood that for a while. But sometimes the heart has its own logic, even when it doesn't make sense in any other way." She paused and looked hard into my face. "I suspect you already know this from other cases."

I did, but it didn't always help. "Does it make more sense now, looking back from this distance, or less?" I already felt how awkward it was to ask her this on the day of Edward's memorial service, but I had her in front of me and I meant to take advantage of it.

Rocio stopped and looked down the row. Next to us was a sculptural display, a grave with a headboard like an old bathtub set upright on the faucet end, with the curved and fluted top forming a kind of grotto. It was filled with pictures of the deceased mother and several devotional images. At the bottom stood a statue of the Virgin with her hands uplifted in prayer, her feet set in concrete up to the ankles. Like the occupant beneath her, she was going nowhere, but not fighting it either.

"If it makes sense now it was because I know it was my means of escape from Edward, but I didn't see it that way at the time. I didn't see it as related to Edward, and it felt wickedly compelling, as if quite by accident I had glimpsed something forbidden when I wasn't even looking for it! I knew within seconds of the moment I first saw Ray walk into the room that I would be sleeping with him. I hate to use the word irresistible, because no man has ever been irresistible to me, but it was very close to that. At the time, I mean. That was two years ago."

"Near the end with Edward."

"Yes."

"Then does Ray figure in your book of poems?"

A firm shake of the head met this. "No." A broad gesture of her left hand swept the question away. "Not the one I gave you. That was all about Edward. Ray was never an empty canvas. He was a riot of form and color, one thing blending into another. He was definitely more like an abstract painting. In contrast to the calm, formal mannerism of Edward, Ray was kaleidoscopic."

"What happened to Ray?" I wondered how he could've projected something like that painting image to her. Perhaps in living with Edward she had acquired an artist's vocabulary in her perspective, more than Maya had living with me.

"At about the time I left Edward, Ray also disappeared. Not in the same way Edward ultimately did, I'm sure. Later, I wondered if I had been interesting to Ray mainly, or even only because of Edward and the Veronica. In any case, I never saw him again. I couldn't tell you if Edward did. Probably not, since he knew what had been going on."

"Did you ever think after you left Edward that you might open your door some day to find Ray standing there?"

"Yes, yes I did." Her voice was faint, no more than a whisper soon lost over that raucously silent amusement park of graves. One of her shoulders went up, but I saw no chip on it. "More than once I have thought that, OK? But it didn't ever happen. With him it would never have been a normal appearance like that, you know? Just to show up at my door, knocking or ringing the bell. Hi, how've you been? He would've preferred something far more theatrical, like dropping into the room from the ceiling." Unself-consciously, she laughed aloud this time.

"What did he look like? I don't suppose you have a photo?"

"No. I wish I did. He's about Edward's height, five-nine or so, with a medium build, black hair, and a widow's peak. His skin is slightly darker than mine, probably a tone that's more typical of the Middle East. He has a wide mouth and an eager, intelligent look, as if he is always about to tell you something important. Brown eyes, of course, under thick eyebrows. He also has an artist's hands, both delicate and formidable, like Edward's."

Without thinking I glanced at my own. "Any other special characteristics about him? Moles or scars?"

"Ray has a strong nose, and large ears, but they lay flat against his head. The soft curl in his hair makes you wonder how he might have looked at twenty, and why you weren't there to see it, perhaps one night in a tavern in the Greek islands when you glimpsed him dancing. And yes, he also has a tattoo on the back of his neck, at the base of his skull right below the hairline."

"I see," I said softly, struggling not to react, but still thinking I knew what was coming. "Do you recall what it was, that tattoo?"

"It was an eye facing left, with an eyebrow above

and two lines coming out from the underside, one pointing downward and the other curving toward the back."

"The Eye of Horus."

"Yes, I recognized it as that, too, but Ray had another name for it. I can't recall it now, but the word sounded guttural, like it had no vowels. Perhaps it was Arabic? I'm only guessing."

"Did you ever ask him what that meant, or why he had it?"

"I did more than once, but he wouldn't ever give me a straight answer. He may not have had any straight answers in him, for me at least."

"Did he ever give you the impression that he might have been a member of some group?"

"Like Rotary? Kiwanis? No, he was too self-absorbed for anything like that."

"I was thinking more like a group that was focused on obtaining the Veronica."

"Groups he might be involved with were not something we ever talked about. He never said anything about his family, either."

"Did he ever ask you about the Veronica?"

"Not directly. A couple of times he said things that referred to it, as if he expected me to make some response."

"Did you?"

"Never. I felt the subject was dangerous ground,

given the way Edward was so deep-ended about it. Any-way, what I liked about Ray was that he was so not Ed-ward during that time. He was absolutely his own per-son, and I resisted making connections like that."

Her manner suggested this was about all she had for me. "I can see that. Thank you for talking to me today. I know it was difficult."

"And I know you'll think of more questions. May-be that will be when you're closer to solving Edward's murder." We studied each other in silence for a while be-fore moving closer to the long white wall that edged the street outside. It was a careful look from both of us, and it made me wish I had been connecting with her under different circumstances. Perhaps we could have a conversation some time that was more about her as Rocio Valdez, the person and the poet, rather than as a bit player in the struggle over the Veronica. I also thought I could easily talk to her about painting. She'd al-ready heard about it from Edward and I think she'd be surprised to have my take on it because it would be so different from his.

Almost as a wake-up call, two young children of the flower sellers ran from one side of the entrance to the other, yelling. We moved close enough to the living world again to begin to hear other sounds emerging from it; a car passing on the Ancha with an exhausted muffler and a thumping stereo, a pair of distant sirens intertwining, a sound truck moving up the hill on Cinco de Mayo, barking faintly and futilely in the late afternoon, something about a circus for twenty pesos.

After a long hug Rocio and I paused under the arch of the cemetery gate. I found I wanted to protect her; from what exactly, I couldn't have said. She'd already been invaded in the night. I also wanted to touch her face with my fingertips. Some of this was not relevant to the case.

The flower vendors weren't doing any business and they looked at her hopefully as we drew apart in the street outside the gate. "Just one more thing," I said as she started to turn. I hadn't forgotten what I was about to say, I was only saving it for last to give her something to think about as she walked away. "What was the name on Ray's passport? Unlike with Edward's journals, you must have looked at it."

She gave me a sparkling smile. "Of course I did. I wanted to know who I was in bed with. It was Rayam Hashem." She spelled it out for me.

"Did he ever explain the other name he was using, Raynaud de Chatillon?"

"No, and I never told him I had seen the real name in his passport. As elegant as he was, he always wanted to be called just Ray, as if he didn't need to put on any airs to impress people. He did speak an excellent kind of French, but with a slight accent. It probably sounded to me like my English sounds to you."

In the angular light of that brilliant but fading January afternoon I stared after Rocio Valdez as she walked away from the Panteón gate, studying the rhythm of her long graceful stride until she turned at a small side street in the direction of the Ancha de San Antonio. Of course Maya and Cody had left with my van long before, but I wasn't sorry to have the opportunity of a quiet walk home alone. I could've accompanied Rocio for a while, since our route was the same until we reached Zacateros, where she would turn up Codo, but I wanted to consider her tale without a layer of small talk over it. With the traffic noise of the Ancha it would've been impossible to continue the kind of conversation we'd been having. I started down the street in the direction she had taken five minutes before.

Naturally, my first question was whether Rayam Hashem was the same man who had purchased Edward's saddle. That would have been as much as thirteen months after Rocio saw him last. Had he been hanging about in San Miguel that entire time? I had never noticed anyone of his description in town, so this line of thought told me nothing.

Still, I couldn't help picturing Rocio enveloped in Ray's grasp, his muscular arms enveloping her elegant shoulders, his lips on her flawless skin. Edward's long absences would've left her with ample opportunity to do whatever she felt she had to do to start a new life. She seemed to have been very certain of what she was doing at that time, but less so as the months passed. It was hard to imagine her as merely a pawn in the pursuit of the Veronica. What did that say about Ray's feelings toward her? And if Ray was not the buyer of the saddle, then we had to be dealing with a group of tattooed men, an organization or a brotherhood of some kind. With Edward dead of a double knife wound, and the elderly Baroness Irena Karsky bludgeoned in her Cuernavaca mansion, it was clearly time to go back to the journals. At times they were still my best source of information, even if it was never quite as current as I might wish.

As I continued to walk along in Rocio's path, where I could no longer locate her among the foot traffic once I emerged on the Ancha, it did not escape me that both of the murder victims had been painters.

CHAPTER FOURTEEN

Maya and Cody were still dressed in their memorial clothes as they sat out in the loggia with an open bottle of Chilean red. A third glass, empty, awaited my return. I was still in a pensive mood, and I had taken my time returning. The image of Rocio that had stayed with me was the dismayed look on her face when I first asked about Ray. As I walked in the thought came to me that she might be wondering now whether Ray had killed Edward.

Cody had hung his jacket over a chair, pulled off his tie, and rolled up his starched cuffs. It didn't make him look much more comfortable, only less formal. I sat down, and after fielding a few questions about Rocio's condition, I told them the story of Ray, starting with the mention of his alias in the journals. I was now privately thinking of him as the demon lover, and I included all the nuances I could recall. The passport slipping out of the back pocket of his pants folded over the chair was an effectively startling detail. His real identity had been escaping from its concealment in his clothes. Especially, the widow's peak gave Ray an almost vampire-like appearance, and I recalled Rocio's suggested image of him dropping from the ceiling, although she had mentioned nothing about an unusual prominence of his incisors.

"That sounds like desperation on her part," Maya said, twirling her glass. "A little way into it with Ray, she would've let Edward discover what was going on. She would have dropped some simple clue. Then his reaction would've told her everything she needed to know, whether she should stay on and try to work it out with him or go."

"Is that what you would've done?"

She gave me an elaborate Mexican shrug that was all presentation and style with no content. It revealed nothing to me.

"I suppose that's better than only threatening to take a lover," Cody said with a dismissive wave of his hand. "I do that all the time and no one responds."

"It works better because people don't like to be threatened," Maya said. "What works best is when they suddenly find themselves between the sword and the wall and they didn't expect it. Then it's easier for them to recognize that it's time to do something. Nobody has to sell them on the idea of action. They reach that point by their own."

Off on the winding gravel path through the

foliage I caught sight of Orlando working his way casually in our direction in the shade of the lower leaves of the bromeliads, as if nothing much was going on. I knew he was listening to this conversation as he pretended to search between the pavers for overturned beetles. He operates with a subtle manner for a long-tailed grackle; many of them come on like they have no manners, *mal educado*, as people say here. Simply out for an afternoon stroll, he paused looking up at a point beyond the table where a snippet of fried pork rind or a shelled peanut, lofted into the air, might fall directly toward his waiting beak, already slightly parted and ready. None did this time.

"Rocio didn't see it that way, at least then," I said. "Looking back, she might think that now. But I imagine she got Edward's attention." Maya poured a glass of wine for me. That finished the bottle, but we had a rack of them inside the kitchen that was built in under the counter. Conversations like this were always a business expense.

"Walking back here I was thinking about the neck tattoo and the fact that we now have two suspects who wear it. Or have we only sighted the same man twice? It's just that the long time period between those sightings suggests there were two men. What says the old psychologist?" Cody had been close to his Ph.D. in psychology when he bailed on academe and went to the police academy to become a third generation homicide detective.

"Well, that struck me too, as you related Rocio's story. Worn in that position, it's not like the tattoo is a secret mark. If there is a group of men that all have the same version, going around committing crimes like murder, then they're probably acting from principle. They don't think what they're doing is wrong, so they're not afraid that people might see the emblem."

"That sounds like terrorist psychology," Maya suggested.

"Yes, or similarly, any people with a deeply religious motivation, and therefore a finely developed ability to rationalize what they do."

"Which fits the pursuit of the Veronica," she added. "Many horrors have been committed in the name of religion."

"But Ray still could be that original person of the saddle purchase too," said Cody, emptying his glass at a gulp, "and maybe he got the Eye of Horus on his neck years ago because his sexy blond college girlfriend was a New Age type. Now he's forty-six years old, she went off years ago and married her insurance agent and has four kids on Long Island, and he hates having to explain the tattoo to everyone he meets so he wears turtlenecks most of the time."

"Works for me," I said. "I'd like to hear him

explain it to all of us the next time we catch up with him."

Not that I or any of us had ever seen him, but still, I had the sense that Ray and I would connect one day not far off. México has a substantial Lebanese community. Salma Hayek is part of it, and of course, Carlos Slim. Both have done rather well for themselves. We opened another bottle of red to analyze these issues in more detail.

Later that night I was still restless when we went to bed. Closing my eyes didn't help. While Rocio had not left me in a condition of peace, it was still a state of mind that frequently accompanied the early phases of most cases. Maya kissed me and dozed off quickly, with her face turned away from my thumbnail-sized reading light. Wine can cause her to do that sometimes. I stayed up and paged through the Jericho journals until I settled on this early entry, one of the few that tried to look at the science of the matter:

June 2

I've come across considerable discussion about what material the Veronica was made from. Silk has been widely rejected as too coarse. Apparently the fabric has some degree of transparency.

Three witnesses have said it can be stored in a thimble, which would make transporting or conceal-ing it easy. One question that comes up is why such a light fabric would be used as anyone's veil? And how could it last so many centuries?

One possibility is that it begins life as a superfine fiber extruded by mussels to aid in cling-ing to rocks and other stable marine elements. The ancients were aware of it and used it to make delicate fabrics, finer than any known medium, then or since.

Another property is transparency, for which uniqueness is claimed in this piece, but that's no longer credible. It's done easily enough in Victorian fabrics. I've painted this effect dozens of times. The idea that the image is reversible is a more difficult issue. Even looking through both faces of the fabric, the image should remain facing the same edge. If these texts are suggesting that when you flip it over the face is turned to the opposite edge to remain unchanged, then we have a problem with reality.

Indeed. Still, I was happy to see Edward recog-nize reality, even to this limited degree. To me, whatever some of these marginal characteristics were, this did not seem like a fabric strong enough to survive interleaved within a chair seat or a saddle, which suggested that the

Eye of Horus people were not well versed in the proper-ties of the treasure they were pursuing. But if they were killing people to retrieve the Veronica, how could they afford not to know what it was?

CHAPTER FIFTEEN

In the morning I went up to the studio to stretch a new canvas. Maya had gone riding again at Rancho Camarena. I knew I needed to apply a few more finishing strokes to the landscape, but I couldn't decide what they were. When that happens it's better to go on to something else for a while and return with fresh eyes a few days later. I pulled all the drapes open and let the sun stream in to warm the tile floor.

Glancing at the newly sketched in landscape of Pozos, it didn't move me and I pulled it off the easel and turned it against the wall. The Mazilu had gotten me thinking about portraits again, and while I didn't have a subject picked out yet, I started setting up a twenty-four by thirty inch canvas just to be ready when I found someone. For this I used a finer weave of linen than I usually favor, since portrait detail doesn't work as well on coarse surfaces. My normal canvas is like burlap under a white primer coat.

It occurred to me that I might see if Rocio

wanted to pose for kind of an uptown head and shoulders, but that seemed way too complicated with everything else that was going on. Even so, I'd love an opportunity to paint her; I found her face compelling.

Taking a break after I had the canvas tacked on and tightened up with corner wedges, I moved over to the Mazilu and studied the eyes of the *Madonna in a Venetian Costume*. The eyes and ears are usually the toughest parts of a portrait, aside from the teeth, and Mazilu has an easy and natural way with both of them. His eyes in particular are always fluid and alive, translucent and full of reflected light. In this case, no ears were visible since they were covered by the Madonna's long hair, but the eyes were vivid and clear. They invited the viewer to peer deeply into them. As I did I was shocked to observe a feature I knew wasn't there. On the mirror-smooth canvas I could now see minuscule ridges of paint on the transitions from one color to another. Almost too slight to detect by touch, they still were apparent to my painter's eyes.

Deeply troubled, I lifted the picture off the wall and held it edgewise to the light slanting in from the windows along Quebrada. I had studied this portrait in detail within the last few days and admired the faultlessly smooth character of the surface, which was almost reflective in its level of polish. Now I could detect extremely faint ridges of paint all over the fine-grained canvas where none had existed before. Was the curling line of the model's lower lip also off by a bit? In a subtle way, her hairline seemed to be handled differently too, it seemed with a little less freedom. On close inspection it also displayed microscopic ridges.

I turned it over. The paper seal covering the back looked just as it did before, and it still bore no gallery imprint. But along the outer edges, where the paper ended and the ultrafine linen fabric had been trimmed to the stretcher line, the treatment at the corners was subtly different. Where the fabric is mitered and tacked down it provides an area that works like an unconscious signature for anyone stretching a canvas, whether artist or gallery technician. I could clearly recall how it had been before, because I noticed it was not the way I do it, and the one I was holding now had been done in yet a third fashion by a different hand.

I turned it over again. The frame was identical, and it could have been the original, where only the painting had been switched.

I had no option but to conclude the Mazilu I held in my hands was a forgery. A first class forgery indeed, and although not perfect, it was certainly worthy of Edward Jericho's subtle brush. You would have to know the nuances of the original as well as I did to spot it, but I wasn't able to think of anyone else who could come this close in reproducing my Mazilu.

As I set the painting on the desk and leaned it against the wall I sat down and noticed that my skin had become chilled all over. It had a prickly feel as if I'd suddenly realized I was in danger myself. Although the studio was still cool I'd started to perspire. There was no doubt that this painting was Edward's work, since he could've worked from the original, but that only opened the door to a dozen other questions.

What had happened to the real Mazilu? Why had Edward painted a copy of this picture when he had possessed the genuine version himself for several years before his death? It struck me that because it was his most valuable picture, he may have hung the fake on his wall during his extended absences and hidden the real one in a vault somewhere. That would explain why the original was still on his wall at his death; he had never intended to disappear that day.

But how had the switch in my studio been made? Maya and I would've noticed signs of a break-in. People might possibly come over the roofs on these houses that share common walls all down the block, as most do in San Miguel, but we always lock the doors on the garden side of the house too at night or when we're going out, and there had been no tampering that we'd observed. So where was my Mazilu, the one I had paid more than two thousand dollars for?

The only time Maya and I had been absent from

the house simultaneously in the last few days was during the memorial service, but Rigoberta, our housekeeper, had been there during that time. She had been my housekeeper since before Maya moved in with me. There was absolutely no question of her honesty. I could've left stacks of thousand-peso notes all over the house and she would've sorted them in order of serial number and squared up the edges, but every one would still be there when she left. I called her cell.

When she answered we went through the usual courtesies. It was always an honor, she said, to be called by one of us. How could she help? I could see her standing there in her floral print apron, which I had never seen her without. I believe it was part of her identity as much as part of her wardrobe.

"Did we have any visitors while we were gone yesterday?" I asked her in an offhand tone.

"Well, no guests as such, Señor Zacher, because of course I would have told you. Only the delivery person from Galeria Uno was bringing one of your paintings back for a small repair."

"Did you look at it?"

"No, it was in the flat box he carried with him."

This was the gallery where I show exclusively in San Miguel. Deliveries or pickups from them were not uncommon at all since we liked to move the inventory around and there were occasional dings from handling to be repaired. "Where did he leave it?"

"He didn't, because he said he couldn't wait so long for you to return, and he had to explain the repair while you were looking at it. But don't have any worries, Señor Zacher, he will call you about it later when he comes back this way."

"How big was this picture?"

"Not big at all. Small like the new one in your studio."

"Did he wait upstairs?"

"*Sí*. He wanted to see what you were working on, as in the past."

"What did he look like?"

"Well, he was shorter than you, with wider shoulders, and with black hair and a pirate beard." By this I knew she meant a full beard.

"I don't suppose you noticed whether he had any tattoos?" This was followed by a moment of silence. "I am thinking of on the back of his neck."

"No, Señor Zacher. I did not see that. Next time I will look."

"Thank you, Rigoberta."

"*Por nada. No hay problema.*"

I saw no need to call Manuel Rivera, who owned Galeria Uno. He wouldn't have any idea what or who I was talking about.

It's axiomatic in the detective business that any

encounter contains information, intended or not, and of varying degrees of value, so I started a list of what this one had told me:

1. They (the other side) knew we were going to be gone for Edward's memorial service. Hence they are somehow connected to Edward, since there was no public announcement, only private invitations.

2. They knew Galeria Uno was in the habit of bringing my paintings back and forth. This practice was not unique to them. I think that almost any gallery does this.

3. They either knew Rigoberta was going to be present at that time to let them in (but how would they know that unless they had watched the house?), or they were taking a chance and would try again if they didn't get in.

4. They knew that the Mazilu was either worth between $2,150 (what I paid) and $10,000 (what Edward had probably paid), or that it was worth far more because it contained an item that Edward and the Eye of Horus people had been pursuing for years. They probably *were* the Eye of Horus people.

5. They knew they could now stop ripping other people's chair seats and saddles apart, since they had easily won this round.

Altogether, what they knew about me was far more than I was comfortable with. I suppose I should've guessed that Edward had copied the Mazilu. What hadn't he copied? And what I had just learned about my own approach to this case was that I probably had been the custodian of the Veronica myself ever since the auction. To believe this was a leap, but I didn't need to thumb through the Jericho Journals looking for my name and what I had been thinking in order to conclude this. If I'd had a badge, it would now be time to turn it in to the director of the Paul Zacher Agency, Maya.

After I'd been stewing about this for nearly two hours the boss returned. By then the only way I had thought of to get on top of all this was to try to join the other side and get a certain neck tattoo myself in order to apply for membership.

She paused just inside the door of the studio. "So you are looking kind of grim today?"

I told her the story of the switched Georges Mazilu painting. I think she was more upset about someone getting into our house so easily than the theft of the picture. Although she liked it, she had never understood it the way I did and when I showed her the copy she could see no difference from the original. For her it was a wash, aside from the monetary value.

For me it was a particularly gross kind of defeat. Maya hadn't immediately guessed that it held the Veronica behind the canvas, and since I wasn't sure of that, I didn't bring it up. The loss of the painting itself was enough to cope with for now. While events like this don't ever make me panic, they do make me angry, and I prefer not to work with an attitude. Attitudes at work are what you get from your garbage man or your bus driver, not your detective.

We stood there in silence for a moment as she studied the picture. Finally she said, "So now I am wondering where was this Mazilu copy during Edward's auction?"

CHAPTER SIXTEEN

The San Miguel City Morgue is a nondescript one-story addition at the rear of the General Hospital, positioned there as if it could be a handy exit for many patients passing through, or merely passing on. Some have said that it looks like an afterthought, although the construction style is a decent match. It is not, however, normally a gathering place for friends on a chilly morning in early February, or at any other time. Few buildings in San Miguel display a more determinedly utilitarian look. The four identical windows facing the parking area are barred, although no inhabitant has ever been caught trying to escape, and little is stored inside that could be pawned or sold. Most Mexicans prefer to shun dead bodies, and there is no black market trade with spare parts in this town.

The morgue is most commonly a place of transition between old and new: a way station where active life is now part of the past, but the residents have not yet been released into a more hospitable eternity at the

Panteón.

The Paul Zacher Agency had been summoned there on only one prior occasion, also by Diego Delgado. It was on the case we filed early last year as *The Girl from Veracruz*, and it was there we were introduced to our late client.

This time the call came to me at 9:45 in the morning. It was only a scant three days after the memorial service for Edward, and Diego Delgado must have been working earlier than usual. He asked if we would like to come down to the morgue and try to recognize a body that had come in overnight with no identification. He felt there was reason to believe it was a murder victim connected with the death of Señor Eduardo Hericho. In view of all the time that had passed, Maya and I both felt this was far from likely, but we were not in a frame of mind to ignore any possible evidence. Furthermore, Delgado had been critically helpful so many times in the past that we had no thought of second-guessing his invitation. I called Cody immediately and he met us on our doorstep ten minutes later.

As we pulled into the five-space morgue parking strip, vacant but for Delgado's official car, a taxi rolled in next to us. Rocio Valdez got out at the same time we did, disentangling her long legs from the back seat of the green and white Nissan. Overhead, the sky was a solid dull steel gray, a depressing backdrop that enhanced nothing around us. The not quite foggy air still hung thick and unmoving among the cluster of unadorned official buildings. Little about them tried to relate specifically to any aspect of San Miguel; we might almost have been in Michigan.

"Licenciado Delgado called me too," Rocio said, shaking hands with all of us after the standard round of greetings.

No one shows up at the morgue without an invitation, and the tour buses never stop there. She was wearing a tan suede jacket with a fleece lining. Like Maya, she had her collar turned up. Her tall boots were a shade of brown that matched the jacket.

"Did he tell you anything when he called?" Cody said. Meaning anything more than he told us, I thought.

"No, only that a man's body had been found and he believed it was related somehow to Edward. He wouldn't say how."

"We're not sure it is related," said Maya. As an upper class Mexican from the capital she was quicker to question Delgado than Cody and I were as gringo expats. Our status always made us more careful of the police.

"I had the idea that he might be trying to find out what we know and this is a convenient pretext to quiz us," I added. But having said that, I wondered if his level of subterfuge would go that far. I felt like we might be underestimating him, but none of us on either side had probably come up with much new information.

We passed through the double doors at the front of the building. The man at the desk asked us all to show our IDs and sign in, and beyond we walked through a second set of doors into the stainless steel and ice blue economy lighting of the cold room. The buffed concrete floors reflected an uneasy brown and ocher glare, the color of old motor oil frozen and polished. An edgy scent on the air offered death and disinfectant in equal parts. Diego Delgado, wearing a lab coat over his brown suit, stood next to one of the drain tables where a body was draped by a blue sheet. Only the bare feet were visible. From one of the protruding toes hung a manila tag on a string. It was turned the wrong way to read, but still, it reminded me of how people hate to be labeled, even in life. Perhaps even less now.

"My best good morning to all of you and I thank you for taking the time to help me out today." Delgado's smile was grim and tight.

"What have we got here?" said no nonsense Cody, stepping a bit closer to the table than the rest of us cared to. We were clustered together a meter behind him.

"Since you are of this case too, I can tell you the victim is a man of mid to late forties, possibly Mexican, although I cannot be sure of that. He was killed from two stab wounds to the back on the left side, just as was

Señor Hericho more than a year ago. This is why I called you here today, although more than this we cannot say, since there is no way to compare the wounds." He spoke rapidly, as if to be sure of getting it all right.

"Where was this body discovered?" said Cody, always calmer than Delgado, routine in his manner but without seeming icy. He had a way of appearing sympathetic without being directly involved.

"It was found lying face down in the small *privada* off the Aldea entrance at four o'clock this morning."

The Aldea is a gated community at the intersection of Zacateros and Codo, where San Antonio ends.

"The Rinconada de la Aldea?" said Maya. "Behind Café Monet?"

"Yes, but further down toward the other end."

This was no more than a passage for foot traffic fronted by a few steps at the upper entrance. "Time of death?" I said.

Delgado met this with a small shrug. "Between midnight and two AM, possibly. It was a cold night and how much time the body spent outside before it was brought to be placed in the *privada* would have some effect on this estimate."

"You don't think this man died where he was found?" said Maya.

"No, since there was no blood flow at the scene, only the very little that had rubbed off on the pavement

185

from the shirt when still wet."

"Did you recover the knife?" I said. He shook his head.

"No witnesses?" Cody said.

"No witnesses that we have discovered yet. The body was found just inside the barricade that forbids cars by a young man heading to work at the Real de Minas Hotel. I will show you the victim's face when you can be ready?"

I thought it was considerate of him to check our preparedness. I glanced at Rocio, wondering whether she had ever attended a meeting like this before. Her arms were clenched tightly over her chest and she wore an apprehensive look with her lips compressed into a straight line. Her expression suggested determination more than fear. Maya was similarly gripping her elbows through the quilted fabric of her white puffy coat with the faux fox collar. Having done many of these morgue visits in Illinois, Cody stood stolidly at one side, his hands relaxed at his sides. Delgado's fingers paused for a second or two while he glanced at each of us, then he pulled the sheet down to the shoulders of the corpse. I think we had all known when we walked in that from the size and appearance of the feet that the victim was not a woman.

Rocio's gasp fell between groan and wail. She spun away, pressing her hands to her face over her open mouth. Maya glanced briefly at the corpse and moved quickly to Rocio's side and put her arm around her waist. Cody caught my eye. I hadn't moved. His lips formed the word *Ray*, and his eyebrows went up.

"Does the victim have a tattoo on his neck?" he said to Delgado.

Cody and I stepped forward as Delgado with his white sterile gloves turned the dead man's head. There in bluish black ink was the Eye of Horus with the eyebrow just edging the hairline. He moved the head back to its original position.

With closed eyes, the dead man's expression was unemotional, as if death had come as no surprise. There was the widow's peak Rocio had described to me, and the thick black hair with no sign of gray. The wide mouth within a thick beard, perhaps once friendly and expressive, was now slightly open and neutral, the large ears nearly flat against the head. So close on the heels of Edward's memorial service, I found this hard to take. Even without knowing the victim, it was too painful and I turned away from it, feeling that whatever evidence this corpse offered was not going to help us solve Edward's death.

I've seen other corpses in this business, many more than I wished to. Still, meeting the dead in this brushed stainless steel room, lying draped on a long tray with raised edges and a drain at the bottom, has an incontestable finality like no other. The presentation is all function and no feeling, and the length of that tray, designed to accommodate someone six-foot-six or more, suggested this corpse was only a minor league death. It was at once unfair and demeaning to the victim.

In my experience, dead bodies even look better lying on the street, molding themselves face down against the well-worn contours of the cobblestones, with the random perforation of the grit and gravel on their faces, like shotgun pellets caught beneath the skin. Their profile at least expresses the character of their final fall. It is a resolution of sorts; this is how it ended, it says. In contrast, this once living body before us had now become no more than an object, a lab experiment offering physical clues or evidence or DNA. I could only shake my head, recalling how Rocio had once found something more than a little compelling about this man, the vibrancy of his colors in life. He was nearly irresistible, she had said. My last thought about Ray alive had been the image of him lying in her arms.

"So you think you might know him?" said Delgado to Cody, or to all of us.

"I will let Señorita Valdez make the identification," I said with relief that someone else could do it much better than I could, since I had never met the victim. Delgado moved past my elbow and spoke to her quietly, with his hand on her shoulder. Rocio looked rigid. As I waited for her reaction I realized I was digging my fingernails into my palms, and I opened my hands and spread them out in front of me, suddenly looking like I wanted to hold this scene at a distance.

"Do you wish to view the body more closely to be certain, Señorita Valdez? Because sometimes, in death, the look of the face will change slightly from the normal, like a relaxation of…" His head rocked back and forth as if to say this effect could go one way or the other. This sensitivity was lost on her.

Rocio shook her head and closed her eyes, then shook her entire upper body from the hips on. "That's Ray lying on the table. Rayam Hashem."

"Surely not a Mexican name?"

"No, Lebanese."

"But you are certain of this, Señorita Valdez?"

She nodded silently. Now her fingers were pressed against her eyes as if to seal them against any further offenses of this kind.

From an inner pocket Delgado pulled out a note-pad and wrote this down. "I would like to invite all of you now to accompany me back downtown for a conversation in a more comfortable place. Perhaps with everyone's contribution we can develop a direction of enquiry better there." He made a subtle motion to an attendant who'd been waiting at the front doors.

"Before we leave I'd like to examine the entry wound," said Cody, "if that is permitted?" This was a courtesy required both in Mexican manners and because Delgado had the official status there. The two walked back to the body as the rest of us hurried outside. The parking lot was about the same temperature as the cold room, but still, it was more inviting. As I paused at the base of the steps I turned to see Delgado pulling out the dead man's hands too, with Cody leaning over to study the nails. The attendant got up and closed the double doors after them, as if to screen a private moment. Two or three minutes later they emerged, and Delgado asked Rocio to ride downtown with him.

There will be no thought of Rocio comparing notes with the Agency on the way, I noted, as the rest of us got into the van.

"Now it's clear that the whole Veronica story is going to come out," Cody said as I pulled into the street.

"Perhaps not the entire story," I said. After reading so much of the journals I now felt like the resource person on this case, in spite of all the passages I had deemed private and skipped.

"What was the knife wound like?" Maya said to Cody.

"Not quite four centimeters wide at the two entry wounds, so about an inch and a half at the top of the blade. Assuming it went in all the way, since the two entry wounds were the same, the knife was not quite long enough to protrude from the front, so eight or ten inches in length."

"Still, a big blade," I said. "Not a switchblade, or one to carry around in your pocket." We passed the Tuesday Market grounds, silent today, the empty concrete slabs windswept, chill, and deserted. They easily reflected the dull gray of the sky. Battered plastic bags wrapped themselves around the base of the steel poles, seeking an end to their aimless travels. "Could it have been the same knife that killed Edward?"

"Hard to tell. But the blade is big enough to leave the same kind of marks on two adjacent ribs going in, as that earlier knife did. Anything beyond that is speculation. Edward left so little physical evidence behind after all that time in the ground."

"A reluctant witness," Maya said.

I skirted the *glorieta* at the Real de Conde and drove down the Querétaro road toward *centro*. "I wonder if Rocio was more upset about Ray's death than about Edward's?" I said, as I turned down San Francisco toward the *jardín* a few minutes later. This route would take us past Rocio's apartment. From the journals, I had earlier described to both of them the downward spiral of her relationship with Edward toward the end.

"But she didn't see Edward's body within hours of his death," said Cody, raising a finger in the air. "She never saw him at all. That makes a big difference. Seeing Ray in the morgue like that has a lot of shock value."

"If you want to call that a value," said Maya from the back seat. "It's never been one of mine."

Cody always needed the legroom of the front. She sometimes found more mental room in the back, as she did now.

I parked in the Recreo lot and, crossing the *jardín*, we walked over to Delgado's office on the second floor of the old Presidencia. Climbing those hollowed and hallowed marble stairs always reminded me of the generations of revolutionaries, bureaucrats, and miscreants that had tread those same steps. From the colony of New Spain, the nation of México had been conceived in this building in 1810 and born over the next eleven years on the field of battle. It had been a difficult and long drawn out delivery.

Licenciado Delgado rose to meet us as we came in. He had not removed the jacket of his brown suit. I had never seen him work in his shirtsleeves, although there must have been times in summer when he did. Rocio was already sitting beside his tacky desk on a straight wooden chair. It was seating for a suspect, as she fidgeted beneath a ceiling fan that hadn't worked in three years, not that anyone needed it that morning. For a woman whose easy composure and grace were two of her best features, she looked like she had lost her way this morning.

Delgado led us into a small conference room at

the back corner that was faced with glass on two sides. "Thank you for coming today. Water for anyone before we start?" He paused with his hand on the inverted forty-liter bottle on a stand in the corner, but no one asked for any.

At Delgado's prompting Rocio began a lengthy narrative of her relationship with Edward, and her later acquaintance with Ray. It soon appeared to be a sanitized version more suited to a family magazine, but one lacking any suggestion of marriage or kids. Nor was there much drama, even towards the end. She composed herself as she developed this with no trace of irony, and sat with her hands folded on the table. The Veronica search was a prominent part of this story, as it had to be, although she did not mention Edward's journals. I was relieved at this because I wasn't ready to give them up to anyone. Even more, I didn't want Delgado to know I was withholding them from him after my pledge of cooperation. So far I hadn't seen anything in them that would help him. They'd surely been of little help to us in terms of the murder, either.

Nor did Rocio suggest that her connection with Ray was anything but friendly and almost professional. They might have been colleagues cooperating in a Notre Dame Ph.D thesis or a Vatican Library query, centered on his mutual scholarly interest in the Veronica, which seemed to have provided a framework for a number of cordial but serious meetings among the three of them. It almost sounded like an obscure academic research group focused in depth on an arcane, but important, artifact. I watched Delgado scanning her performance for flaws. I didn't see any myself, but I didn't know his methods of making judgments of that kind, and I could only see her face in profile.

When she finished, Maya and Cody and I took turns relating the little we knew, which was all second-hand, since none of us had ever seen Ray alive. When we had finished, Delgado continued to make notes for a while, biting his upper lip, then scooped the papers up, aligned the edges, and set them at the corner of the table. I had a sudden idea, but Delgado spoke before I could.

"I have just one more thing." As if this were a casual afterthought, he reached into the inner pocket of his jacket and withdrew a small manila envelope, about two inches by four. From observing him in earlier cases, I knew from his interrogation style that this would contain his hole card. Everyone stared at it as an uneasy silence fell over the table. With a frown, Cody was brushing his lower lip with his thumbnail. Our collective narrative had contained so many careful omissions that we were all vulnerable to a surprise, yet the physical evidence in this case had been so sparse it was hard to imagine what Delgado could've come up with.

"I discovered this item in Señor Hashem's pants

pocket, although his wallet was gone when we found him. It does not look very current, yet I can't help feeling it must have some relationship to this case."

With the nail of his index finger he opened the unsealed flap. A skeleton key, rusty and well worn, slid out onto the table. A flicker of dismay subtly crossed Cody's face, but Delgado was staring at Rocio, as I was. From my angle to her face I saw no change of expression, only that her eyes showed more motion than was required to focus on the key. Next to me, Maya squirmed slightly on her chair. "Do you know this key, Señorita Valdez?"

"I have never seen it before," she said, after an uncomfortable pause.

Why would she pause like that? I thought. She either recognized it or she didn't. Yes or no would've been good enough. In this business people who hesitate or explain too much quickly lose credibility.

Delgado regarded her in the way a coyote might focus on a plump barnyard hen after a fruitless day of hunting in the barren hills. "Perhaps you could show us your apartment key now."

"That's not it." She lost no time in saying that. "I know I still have it, since I used it to lock up this morning when I left." Rocio reached into her small purse and pulled out a similar skeleton key linked to a bronze medallion. It was in much better condition than the one on the table and still bore a few traces of a polished surface. Delgado took it from her and compared the profile of the two against the light, then passed them around the group.

"I have already lifted the victim's fingerprints from this key. It held no others. You may all handle it."

This was an unnecessary gesture, unless he was trying to call her out in front of all of us to give it a bigger impact. But for the degree of wear, the two keys were a perfect match. He shrugged as if this were a mere detail that he had long ago foreseen. Even without a dusty sombrero, there had been moments in the past when he reminded me of a Mexican villain in a B grade 1940s western movie. This was another one of them. He cleared his throat.

"But I know this already because while we were at the morgue, I sent our Officer Peña to your apartment to try it out, from only by a guess. You will understand there are few buildings in our small city that still use these old locks, nine to be exact, all grand casas from the ancient days. When I saw this key come from the victim's pocket I wondered if there was not some relationship there that had continued after Señor Hericho disappeared. This is how I think from the evidence." He placed two fingers to the left side of his head as if that was the area where ideas of this kind originated.

Rocio shook her head firmly, her lips tight. "That is not the case. I never saw Ray again after Edward disappeared." While this skirted the point, I had no trouble believing it.

Here Cody leaned across the table and placed his hand on Delgado's cuff. "You have been very skillful in discovering this, but here are the facts of what happened. Not long ago Paul and I were called to Señorita Valdez' apartment in the early morning hours. An intruder was inside, she told us. There had been no forced entry, but she had heard someone moving about inside."

Delgado stretched out both hands as if this were difficult to understand. "But she did not call me then? I had already talked to her."

Maya leaned toward his shoulder. "I'm sure you were off duty. There may also be an issue of trust here, Licenciado. Did you not tell her you believed she might have killed Edward Jericho?" For his benefit, she now pronounced this as *Hericho* too.

Delgado's eyebrows went up, as did both hands. "Of course, but I would say that to anyone, only to see the reaction, do you know this? That is how we work."

"Do you mean you don't really think I killed him?" said Rocio, nearly sputtering in a tone of growing irritation. I would've thought she'd be relieved.

"Well, possibly, but who can know this for certain? With what little you are all telling me there are many gaps yet remaining to be filled. I have never known so many nice and harmless people as you have described today."

"Aren't there other ways Ray could have gotten that key if Rocio didn't give it to him?" said Maya, with a growing degree of indignation that she was struggling to contain.

With no shortness of breath, Diego Delgado could execute the Mexican shrug at the Olympic level, and he chose this moment to demonstrate that. "Well yes, anyone can buy these keys by the bucket for seventy-five pesos at the Tuesday Market. At one time all the houses in this town used them. Now they are mainly employed in making the new jewelry of esteampunk, the style is it called? Perhaps you have seen this, with old parts instead of new throughout. Gears from old watches and so on."

"And using no precious metals," said Maya, nodding.

"No. Yes! So you do know this? I am right! My wife is making this now for sale with the artisans at the Instituto Fair."

Maya gave him a focused look as she placed both hands flat on the table. "So let's pull this together. You are saying that the victim must have gone to the market, bought a bucket of skeleton keys, and tried them at Rocio's door when she was not home only to get in later at night. But if he found the right one, as he seemed to, why not use it to get in then?"

Delgado was not disturbed by this question.

"Maybe he wanted to get her too? Who can read his intentions so early in this case?"

"Or maybe he only tried them that night," I suggested, feeling this track was pointless. From what I already knew it seemed that Ray wouldn't have had to break in to reconnect with Rocio, even if her view of him had evolved with time.

Glancing at her I could see she was struggling too with the idea that it had been Ray who broke into her apartment, and how that fit into her prior relationship with him. Two years had passed without contact with Ray. She had not seen the intruder. Why hadn't he said hello? Rocio leaned forward toward Delgado.

"Why couldn't it only be a coincidence that Ray had that key? Maybe he was staying in another old house like mine? Isn't there a limit to how many patterns there can be with keys like that?"

"That's why no one uses them now," said Cody, nodding. "They originated at a time when not everyone could afford mechanical locks, which at first were all handmade and expensive, so the number of patterns in use was much smaller."

"There is also one more thing," said Maya. "A saddle belonging to Edward Hericho was purchased at Rancho Aria by a man with a tattoo like the one we saw this morning." Delgado's eyebrows went up, his lips pursed, as if he had just snapped at something passing by and missed.

"And when did this happen?"

Rocio turned away with a pained look. She hadn't heard this before.

"About seven months after Edward disappeared. If you send a man around with a photo of the deceased and talk to Rodrigo the groom and Señora Montgomery-Kingman we might find out if more than one man has that tattoo."

Delgado nodded slowly. "I will send Officer Peña to the rancho this afternoon. Are you suggesting a conspiracy?"

Only a conspiracy of confusion and cross-purposes, I thought. "Please let us know what you find out." I said, suspecting Phaedra might be more forthcoming about the names and dates of that sale when confronted by a police officer. More than she had been with Maya, anyway. Phaedra had, after all, received the money from the buyer and given him a receipt before sending him on to Rodrigo, despite her disdain for anything that reeked of "trade."

"Then I believe we are finished," Delgado said, spreading his hands apart as he looked around the table. "Unless…?"

"There is one more thing." I drew out my cell and pulled up the three footprint shots I'd taken outside Rocio's building on the night of the invasion. "These could be clearer, but the images were drying fast when I took them. They still might be a match for Rayam Hashem's shoes. I assume you have his clothing here?" From a previous case, I knew that a murder victim's clothing was boxed up and sent from the morgue to the evidence room downtown immediately.

Delgado looked at me as if I might have added a centimeter or two to my detective stature, which often appeared to him somewhat less than my natural height. Rocio leaned over my arm and looked at them, then turned away without comment.

"I'll send these to you now," I said.

We spent another eight or ten minutes circling a progressively smaller patch of ground. None of us offered anything of real interest beyond what we'd said, although I clarified the circumstances of the photos and why the shoes were wet. Delgado did not uncover the fact that Ray and Rocio had been lovers, despite her reaction at the morgue. Her response may not have been uncommon in that situation, and could've come from a variety of relationships with the deceased.

At home, in the late afternoon of that day, I received a call from Delgado with the name of the saddle buyer. I didn't ask him what it took to pull this information out of Phaedra Montgomery. The name was Raynaud de Chatillon, which meant nothing to him. I told him it was an alias for his morgue victim, Rayam

Hashem. The shoeprints, although vague on the detail, were a clear match in both design and size for the shoes Ray had been wearing when he died. Although, Delgado added, with the edges so blurred, you couldn't prove those prints came from his pair of shoes specifically.

But what were the odds that they hadn't?

CHAPTER SEVENTEEN

N one of us were happy that the first suspect we'd turned up in Edward's murder was already dead before we could talk to him. Worse, that was the only way we would've found him, since we had no idea that Ray was even still in town, or that he had returned.

The day after our morgue visit I considered calling up Rocio and trying to probe her a bit further, but it didn't seem like she'd be ready for it, given what she'd been through between viewing Ray's body and the visit to Delgado's office. I knew she was still stewing over the meaning of the wet footprints and the duplicate skeleton key. Nor could she have been reassured that Delgado had so lightly accused her of Edward's murder. By now she probably had more questions for me than I had for her. I sensed she was getting tired of hearing about this case, of constantly bumping against the rough edges of it, but her relationship with both Edward and Ray allowed her no escape from it. At the core of Edward's lifestyle and search for the Veronica were all those other issues about his relationship with Rocio. Maya may have been getting tired of it too, and not getting paid for any of our time would've been part of her dwindling enthusiasm.

Back up in the studio pretending to paint that morning, a hopeful activity that often precedes real painting, but not always, I also found myself distracted, since I was trying not to mutter as I glanced at the Mazilu copy every five minutes. I would've pulled it down and stuck it in the storage cabinets if I hadn't thought it still had something to tell me.

I'd been listening to a Maria Callas recording of Donizetti's *Anna Bolena,* possibly as a way of getting inspired to work. What I love about Callas is that she often took big chances. In addition to her best performances she could sometimes sound like a chicken in the distress of laying an oversize egg. This always reminded me of painting, of going for an effect that was a stretch and not always pulling it off. Consistency in painting occurs mainly when the unsatisfying outcome will still be on the canvas waiting for me the next day. When the doorbell rang at about eleven o'clock, I wasn't expecting anyone.

Maya had gone out again to Rancho Camarena and I was not in a chatty mood. With the loss of the Mazilu, it seemed that for every step we'd taken forward, we had taken two steps back. Thinking the

person at the door might be a neighbor wanting to bor-
row a cup of gin, or another phony delivery from Galeria
Uno, I slipped impatiently downstairs without turning
off the music. There I opened the door to discover Dillon
Gericault with his finger poised rigidly in the air as if
about to either press the bell again or raise an important point. I had shaken his hand briefly at the memorial,
but our conversation had gone no farther than a polite
exchange of condolences. I wasn't sure he remembered
who I was. Now I shook it again and asked him to come
in. The shabby way I was dressed and the need for some
mental preparation with a potential client were two
reasons we wanted most people who call at the Agency to
have an appointment.

Dillon was wearing crisp khakis with a careful
crease and a long-sleeved pale green shirt with a navy
vest over it. A sleek pair of mesh Ecco trainers flattered
his feet, suggesting that they worked harder than they
actually did, since he looked too comfortable around
the middle to be an athlete. The weather was warming slightly but not enough for comfort so I didn't ask
him out to the loggia. Instead I led him into the great
room and settled him on the sofa, where the view above
the fireplace was my portrait of Maya dressed as Frida
Kahlo, right down to the unibrow. He stared at it for a
moment, stroking his chin, which was pointed like
Edward's had been. Since this looked like real Agency

business, I wished I wasn't wearing my spotty painting clothes, but I didn't care to run off and change without finding out what he wanted in more detail first. I realized I should've turned off the upstairs music too. Maybe this conversation would be brief, and he was there only to tell me he was going back to New Orleans and he wished me well with the investigation.

"I remember meeting you at Edward's memorial, but I didn't know what business you were in," he began, placing his fingertips together thoughtfully.

"I try to downplay it on occasions like that. How did you find out?" I didn't know which business he meant.

"Well, I knew you were a painter, of course, but what came out this morning was your *real* business. Rocio told me about your painting when I was setting up the guest list, but it was only a half an hour ago that Detective Delgado told me about your detective agency. I came over just now from his office. Maybe I should've called first for an appointment." He eyed my rough clothes uneasily. So did I. You always want to establish a conversation like this on equal terms. This was already strike one and he was pitching.

"If you don't mind my painting clothes, I'm sure it'll be OK." From upstairs I could vaguely hear Maria Callas launching her long aria early in act two, proclaiming her loyalty to the queen she was about to displace in Henry VIII's affections. Callas was always rather breathless near the end. This was my favorite part of the opera. Irony always captures my attention.

I didn't want to correct Edward's brother, but Delgado was not a detective, at least not as stated in his title. He was a prosecutor with investigative duties. Regarding Dillon from the side I was able to get a better idea of his face and manner than I had at the memorial service, where we'd been standing two rows behind him. He was immaculately groomed, and his hair was perfect. He didn't seem ill at ease exactly, although his gestures were slightly vague. It was as if he was looking for a more precise way to express himself in an unfamiliar environment. Did it require a slightly different vocabulary? He seemed more off balance than nervous. If he'd been on stage I would've said that he was playing a character that was not quite a perfect fit for the scene he found himself in. By contrast, Edward had been smooth at nearly everything, except some entries in the journals that referred to Rocio during the final weeks, and of course, the advent of Ray.

"It was Delgado who told me I should talk to you. He said you were also working on Edward's case." Dillon's arm described a vague circle that encompassed nothing in particular. I probably couldn't have been any more precise in defining its boundaries myself. Any time I believe I can accurately mark out the edges of a case, the solution is almost certain to be discovered beyond them.

Covertly I checked my hands for wet paint, although I had barely done any more than squeeze some zinc white out onto the palette. It's the most translucent of the three whites. Without realizing it, I may have chosen it because that was so opposite to any feature of this case. "Did you have a question Delgado couldn't answer?" I delivered this with an encouraging smile. If Dillon did, I could probably add it to my own list of the ones *I* couldn't answer, which was growing in length daily.

"You could say that, but I wanted to hold back for a few days after the service before I talked to the police about this, so it didn't appear unseemly, me being Edward's heir, you know? You can probably see that." As he got further into the subject his voice displayed a more Southern accent. Edward hadn't had one that I could recall.

"Are you suggesting something is missing from the estate?" I wondered how he would know. He didn't attend the auction, which I surely would've if my painter brother had died. I'd have been choosing the pictures to hang on my own walls. Maybe Dillon had somehow found out that Edward's Mazilu copy was not in the auction, but I didn't see how.

"Well, yes, I think you could say something is missing. All of Edward's money is gone." He shook his head slowly.

I let this settle in for a moment, not seeing an obvious link to the case, although one had to be there. Maybe Edward had spent it. Anyone who tries to live by making any kind of art knows it provides a chancy return, although I had always thought Edward could've lived on his painting income. "Were the investments held in the States?"

"Yes, it was in a bank and two brokerage accounts in New Orleans. The statements were among Edward's personal effects. Delgado told me that American banks or investment firms will never give him any information on their depositors or their accounts. That's why he suggested I see you."

"I've also heard that before, although I'm not sure I could do any better. Do the statements show the withdrawal?"

"Well, partially, since the cash, which was about $42,000 in money market funds, went from the bank to the brokerage accounts, and that's clear enough, because you can see it both leaving and coming in. But from each of the brokerage accounts the total withdrawal is merely marked as a 'transfer.' One of the officers told me that since the receiving firm is not mentioned, that meant it went to a confidential account, one that most often would be in a Swiss institution, although it could also mean one of several in the Caribbean islands or Panama. That's a dead end. The brokerage firms all swear to keep information like that secret. If they don't, they lose the privilege of doing business with that bank. Maybe with all of them, I don't know." A note of misery had crept into his face.

"Did you notice whether the brokerage assets were cashed out before they left? In what form did they leave?"

"There was no sign of that on the statements. I think they would've said if they had gone to cash."

"If they were still held in bonds and mutual funds that means they went to another brokerage, rather than a bank, which can only hold cash or mortgages. It could easily have gone offshore."

Here the baritone abruptly broke in from up in the studio, thundering about an issue that had also gotten his dander up. It sounded like the robust Henry VIII himself after a flagon or two of claret and an evening of accelerating regret. Now I wished even more that I had turned the damn sound system off, or at least closed the studio door, because Dillon's voice had gotten lower and more confidential in tone as he went further into this matter.

"Sorry for that noise upstairs," I said. "When did this happen?"

"In November more than a year ago, the month he probably died."

"So you're saying we can't tell whether this transfer occurred before he died or after, only that it was at approximately the same time. What was the date of the transaction?"

"November 14."

"And the amount?"

"Just over one and a half million dollars." He paused a second or two for effect. "What are you thinking?"

"I'm trying to integrate this with the idea of a murder by an intruder, which is how everybody has been looking at Edward's death, including us in the Agency. Like it was a home invasion where the invader encountered the owner unexpectedly, although that was never such a great fit with the careful burial. But still, not everything always dovetails perfectly. We often wrap up a case that still has unexplained details. The money transfer could either be unconnected, or directly connected if the crime was really something else."

I saw no need to mention Ray's murder, even though it was done in the same manner as Edward's. Ray was certainly connected to the Veronica, but we hadn't been able to directly link the Veronica to either of the murders. This new information from Dillon only further muddied the waters.

He leaned forward with his elbows on his knees. "Mr. Zacher, I would like to be blunt if I may."

I made a gesture like Don Corleone in *The*

Godfather, leaning my head to the right as I shrugged. "Go ahead. Life is blunt. Death is blunter."

"Is someone employing your agency to investigate Edwards murder? I hope it's not out of line for me to ask that."

"If it was out of line I wouldn't answer it, but no, we've picked up this case pro bono."

His face expressed no surprise. "Then may I also ask why you would take this on without getting paid?"

Normally Maya would've furnished this answer to a prospective client, but she already had to the rest of us. "Sure, that's the easiest of your questions so far." I leaned toward him for emphasis. "It's because we don't like to see painters murdered. It sends the wrong message. Our response is that you can't get away with it, no matter how valid you think your reasons, and how good you think you are. The Paul Zacher Agency will always be better than you are, and we will take you down, whatever it requires."

I thought this sounded good; it was at once high-minded and principled in a way we could rarely afford to really be in this business as it was practiced day by day in the streets.

I was glad to see Dillon nod as if this made sense. "Then I would like to hire you now. I want your agency to furnish me with all the information you're digging up and I'll be happy to pay for it at your standard rates.

Edward and I were heirs to the same family inheritance. If I may say so, I think I've invested mine more fruitfully. Edward didn't pay as much attention to his; as he painted he mainly wanted to clip the coupons, as they used to say when everybody had bonds and they actually paid real interest. The money to hire your agency is not a problem for me."

"Before I respond, then, you should understand that so far this has been a difficult case for us. As I'm sure Diego Delgado told you, your brother's remains were not in a condition that could provide much physical evidence of the crime. His house had been cleaned up, and the precise location of the murder was never identified. Consider also that by now a lot of time has passed. No witnesses to any part of this investigation have ever come forward. You can understand why we haven't made much progress so far. That could change at any time, but we can never offer a client any guarantees. To tell you the truth, I've been happy not to have a client I had to report to. Until now, of course."

Somehow I felt I had to add that last part. This conversation had become more serious than I expected, and as I spoke I tried to position my gestures to cover the rip in the left knee of my jeans. I'm not usually very formal, but this was a new low in presentation.

Dillon Gericault was shaking his head as I finished. "You're underselling yourself. Inspector Delgado told me that even the idea that Edward had been murdered was an inference your group made merely from the position of the house keys hanging on the kitchen wall during the auction. I thought that was nothing less than brilliant."

"Thank you. That insight came from my partner, Cody Williams."

"But I understand what you're facing here and I don't intend to demand any more than your best effort."

I nodded agreeably. That's all anyone ever got. "You received Edward's personal effects. I believe the landlord shipped them to you some time before the auction team arrived to do the catalogue. Did they appear to be complete?"

It was Dillon's turn to shrug. "Well, nothing was obviously missing, but who could answer that, you know? The normal things were all there. I even have his toothpaste and dental floss, as if that matters now, even though they're the same brands I use. It was just about what I would've expected, but still..."

I don't do trivia well, so I didn't intend this, but I found my index finger was suddenly tapping on the mesquite surface of the coffee table. "Did you find anything among that material that would suggest Edward was being threatened?"

His mouth opened for an instant but he didn't speak. I withdrew my hand from the table as a subtle

silence thickened around us. Even the music paused upstairs. Dillon Gericault leaned forward with his hands
clasped between his knees. His back was arched and his
mouth opened twice before he spoke. Having reached
this point with clients before, which often resembled an
early degree of surrender, but still short of complete
capitulation, I said nothing to rush him.

"Not really, " he said finally.

"But aren't you hesitating when you say that?"
I can still spot the cues, or the tells, as Cody would call
them.

"Well, it's only that I know he kept a journal;
so there could be something relevant in those pages. It
wasn't with his things that were sent on to me, and the
police don't have it. Or if they do, Sergeant Delgado won't tell me. He seemed to not know about
it, if you think you can trust him on that. You would
probably know how to read him better than I could. I
hope you do."

Sensing we were at a tipping point, I studied
Dillon Gericault's face for a while. Whether we would
accept any case was always Maya's call as head of the
Agency, and she had picked some real losers. But this
was one we'd already taken. The only additional issue
remaining was whether we'd be paid for our investigation or not. Sharing our results with the victim's closest
family member and principal heir seemed legitimate to

me. Even more than the rest of us, Maya preferred that the Agency get paid, since she wrote the checks to cover the expenses at the end. While she did this I struggled to write up the final report and Cody cleaned and oiled all our guns, even the bullets, as he switched through the channels looking for a football game.

"OK. The Paul Zacher Agency will take this case. We'll need a $2,000 retainer to start, and after you write that check I'll be able to give you your first piece of client information."

With a satisfied smile, Gericault pulled out a checkbook from a pocket within his vest and began writing with a flourish.

As he handed the check to me, slightly curved under his broad thumb, I said, "I have Edward's journals upstairs. I'm still going through both volumes. The auction staff tossed them in among the art books I bid on."

A broad grin came over his face, pulling his cheeks up higher over the triangular chin to reveal a pair of dimples. "You guys are so damned good! That's what I call quick results!"

"Thank you. Luck matters in these cases too, more than we would like. At times it can even save your life, which is not reassuring at all. My next question is what you know about Edward and his search for the Veronica?"

Dillon leaned back into the cushion with a more

thoughtful expression, nodding. "I know what it is, or what it was, or what it pretends to be, OK? And I know that he was after it for years. Beyond that, I have no more information. Rocio wouldn't talk about it to me. It seemed like she felt it was a sore point between her and Edward before she left him, although I don't know why that would be."

I looked at him for a long moment. "How close were you to your brother, I mean when you were growing up?"

He shook his head slowly. "That was a relationship of chance, you know? Aside from being born as twins, we had little in common growing up. He's the older one, by four minutes, but it was like we had different mothers. And he was always the artsy one, even as a little kid. He would copy the comic strips from the newspaper on his lunch napkin while I played Monopoly and made neat little stacks of the money."

"How do you make your living now?"

"I have a chain of six dry cleaning outlets. Damn good ones, too." What followed was the only truly satisfied look I had seen on his face since he rang the doorbell.

"I see. Then I have only one more question. Can you think of anyone who might have killed your brother, or made off with his money, or both? For example, would he have given his account passwords to anyone he might've trusted too much?"

A frown clouded Dillon Gericault's face as he nodded. "I suspect he might have been a little careless about that. He never liked even the idea of business. I hate to accuse someone without any evidence, but yes, I do have a feeling about that at least. Maybe it's no more than intuition, but I think the person behind *all* of this case is Rocio Valdez. If you know her, you may already have concluded that too. You guys are so far ahead of everyone else on this."

I nodded without comment. We rose and said our goodbyes, parting cordially, but without swearing to remain good friends. Still, Dillon Gericault's suspicions were about ninety degrees off from mine. As he moved down Quebrada toward the overpass I had the sudden thought that Edward may have used some or all of that million and a half dollars to pay for the Veronica. Would he have gone that far to get it?

CHAPTER EIGHTEEN

When I returned to the studio after his departure, during which time Dillon Gericault
had shaken my hand far more than was
necessary, Donizetti's final notes had long faded away,
and I knew that Ann Boleyn had gone to her death both
young and unpardoned for not holding the interest of
Henry VIII. Given the nature of opera, I could imagine
the king's messenger galloping posthaste to the scene, his
horse frothing at the mouth, Henry's last minute change-
of-mind parchment reprieve curled in his hand, but sadly
just a scant moment too late. The ax would have fallen
as the page leapt from his saddle tossing the reins to a
waiting groom.

In any opera I always pay more attention to the
music than to the plot, but this still easily reminded me of
how the injection of Edward's missing fortune into this
case brought with it a peculiarly unsatisfying ambiguity
as to the outcome. No horseman was coming back with
it. Was this case really about the Veronica, or was it now

about his money—a worthy goal in itself? Since Rocio first told me about it, I had always thought of the Veronica as a "celebrity artifact," since the glow of its starry presence could easily overshadow the other elements in an investigation. It's usually a fallacy to assume that when two events happen at about the same time one causes the other, or that they are even necessarily connected. I made a mental note to email Dillon about whether Edward might have had any other potential heirs, and to watch his own back.

It must have tortured Dillon to have to flesh out the memorial service guest list with the help of Rocio Valdez, and then to stand so close to her in the front row, with only the short woman between them. All the while in his mind he must have been seeing Rocio plunging that wide brutal knife blade into Edward's back. Not just once, but knowing how it felt to do it the first time, then to do it again seconds later.

That did not make me think Rocio had killed Ray as well, or either of them. She was a tall and relatively young woman, but dead bodies are floppy and uncooperative, and to have killed Ray and dragged his corpse from a car without assistance into the privada border below Café Monet seemed improbable. Besides, as I already knew, Rocio did not have a car. Using a taxi was also quite unlikely, even though some of them here have the rear cargo box of a small pickup.

Cody had once told me that some murderers often take a grim satisfaction in attending the victim's funeral as a kind of veiled triumph, so the police were always represented there too, scanning the crowd for "tells." But I reminded myself that Dillon had offered nothing but his own intuition to back up his guess of Rocio's guilt, and if he had possessed anything concrete to give it more credibility, he would've had no reason not to share it with me.

I was, of course, ready to admit that I didn't want to believe Rocio had murdered Edward. I've been in this shabby business long enough now so that I can trust my character judgment of people ninety percent of the time, even though I haven't always been right. I decided to go back to the journals, which, in the spate of current developments, I had neglected for a few days. I sat down in my wicker chair and found only one of them at hand. Maybe Maya had glanced at the other one. In the early section of that second volume I came across this passage in Edward's voice:

January 7

The "Acts of Pilate" is one of those apocryphal documents that the Church decided to snub when they were putting together the "real" New Testament for the ages to come. Some sources assign it to the mid fourth century, which would've made it at least a contemporary contender for inclusion. The early church father Epiphanius certainly refers to it in 376. No one can say today why it didn't make the cut, but many other documents that also didn't still raise questions for scholars today.

As Justin Martyr wrote at the time, "And that these things did happen, you can ascertain from the Acts of Pontius Pilate." –The First and Second Apology of Justin, Chapter 35. Clearly that had some credibility at the time.

This document is the earliest I've come up with for a mention of the Veronica in the historical record, and while the early church fathers may have found another argument to drop the Pilate document because of its uncertain origins, they may well have regretted it later, because soon after, the Veronica became HUGE.

With all the time I had spent on the journals, in some entries I still felt Edward was trying to prove something to himself. This passage was one. I began to wonder whether he hadn't been fairly cagey in his construction of these notes, which didn't make sense if they were designed only for his own review. It didn't seem like he'd be teasing himself, yet they tended at times to set up an argument without reaching any conclusion. Was he some kind of tease after all? Was he throwing his own ball into the air only to see whether he could catch it himself every time? It was like cheating at solitaire.

I leaned back in my wicker chair, which always gives off a satisfying fibery creak that sounds like the essence of contentment and relaxation. It was the most comfortable seat in the house. But at the same moment, adjusting my back to the cushion, I abruptly realized how foolish I had been to ignore nearly all Edward's journal references to Rocio Valdez out of some delicate instinct of respecting her privacy in that relationship. Decency has its limits, and they crop up sooner for detectives than for most other decent people. The truth was that I really did want to know why her breasts were so goddamn great, and why she refused to pose nude for him. Why not admit it now? No one but Cody and Maya will ever see these files, and they're both used to my rants.

I had a suspicion that Edward would give me some answers in those skipped-over journal pages, and while he did that, he might also offer some further hints about Rocio's role in this case. Nobody is beyond suspicion, as Cody would say, as he had more than once.

Diego Delgado believed her a suspect, at least enough to raise the question publicly that Rocio might have done the murder, and Dillon's instinct had brought up her name again. This might have come from nothing more than her close association with the victim. Still, how could I continue to ignore all the journal entries about her merely because I didn't want to think she was guilty? To me, she didn't *look* guilty, she didn't *talk* guilty, and she had no motive, but was that in any way a systematic approach to use in a murder case, possibly a double murder case? One where Rocio Valdez had been the lover of *both* victims, and both had now died in an identical manner? Uncomfortably, the term *black widow* came to mind. In the way I'd been looking at it, so far I had done no more than accommodate my own prejudices. I should've recused myself earlier in this case, like right after the auction, but my curiosity had made me go on. A phrase of Cody's came to mind, one he'd used several times. "You know how you are about women; you tend to give them a break they don't deserve sometimes."

My only defense was to say, "Well, not always." It lacked conviction.

With a frustrated sigh I went back into the journals, scanning this time for Rocio's name. Often it was betrayed by a special flourish in Edward's elegant script.

May 6

The out-of-kilter painter Georges Mazilu would so appreciate the irony of having the actual Veronica tucked up against the back of his canvas! I scraped off the paper covering the rear, with its label stamp from Galerie Etrange in Paris. The new sheet of paper I plan to put on will be blank, but who would ever know what's missing? This picture will always be innocently hanging on my wall, silently protecting a relic that caused the death (as close as I can estimate from all the sources I've found) of 34 people. And Rocio believes she knows me so well! Ha! I've had the Veronica for three weeks now and she's never picked up on it for a single moment. But I know what she's been up to with that always so eligible bachelor, Ray! Raynauld de Chatillon. Who was he really? Bill Schwartz? Don Smith? In any case, that's the source of her distraction.

And how could I not instantly recognize the mark on his neck? There are more of them out there, and I have seen them before. They will all be coming after me now, just like they did with Irena Karski. They have a way of knowing what is happening behind the scenes. I don't know how, only that I am smarter than she ever was, even if she did make it to nearly 82. Not a bad painter, though, in her own way and time.

I admit that I read Edward's entry coldly. I feel it still. It was not that I wished him any more ill, but if Edward Jericho was so smart why was he dead? And if I was so smart, why hadn't I looked into the Rocio passages more closely? The entire story had been in my hands since the auction. If I had seen how it went I'd still have both the real Mazilu and the real fake Veronica myself now. I'd be one in a long series of people who'd had it, where thirty-four of them had been murdered before me. Now it was thirty-five with Edward. Or was it thirty-six with Ray? Perhaps possessing the Veronica, or even chasing it, was no blessing. Think of the moonstone or the Hope Diamond.

There is always a temptation among detectives to believe they are smarter than other people. That also can make for a brief career in this business.

Not seeing the second volume nearby, I opened the journal to another place.

May 17,

At other times the painting is not enough, nor is owning the Veronica. Like now, when I'm lost in the night, in the darker, deeper, blackness of these long and naked nights, Rocio is so bleakly gone. Her side of the bed is grown so cold and so withdrawn from me. Its silence testifies against me in dead languages. They possess the rhythm and cadence of life but no meaning. Now I wish I had not been so single-minded about the Veronica, a fleshless filmy thing long dead. Rocio's firm body, her heated skin against mine, her breath on my face, on my neck, and in my ear. That was life. I have always painted the past, worshipped the past in its detail, as if the present offered nothing of interest. In revenge, the present now flees from me, as if the past is approaching on its own, rushing up on violent horses. Out of control, yet as if it owned me. Whatever can it offer now but death? Both the past and the present have deserted me. What remains? Someone will find this, I am sure. But by then all will be lost. It will only be a long translation in a dead language no one cares to study.

What comes next from the night? I think it will be time to move on soon, before they come for me. Ray is only their scout, their outrider. They move in ranks behind him on black horses through the darkness.

After this I found it impossible to get into my painting again, not that I had been deeply engaged before Dillon arrived. As some are, the day was lost, so I started to put my brushes away. I hadn't even gotten as far as squeezing out any other colors of paint after the zinc white. Not much later Maya returned from riding and stuck her head into the studio.

"Finished?"

"More like not even started. Come on back after you change and I'll tell you about our visitor today."

She disappeared into the bedroom to get out of her gear and wash off her sunscreen.

When she returned five minutes later I offered Maya the wicker chair while I sat back down at the easel. Facing her, I lifted the canvas off, set it against the wall, and put my heels up on the cross bar near the base.

I was trying to find a good beginning when she said, "Your guest must have been Dillon."

This took me by surprise. "Why would you say that?"

"Because everyone else in this case is dead, except for Rocio, and she's not likely to show up here. You're usually on her doorstep. Anyway, there were never that many options to start with."

I shrugged. "I do have to go where the information is, and she's been our best source, so far. Anyway, you're right, it was Dillon Gericault visiting."

"I am surprised. You must have been too. Did he make an appointment first?"

"No." I told her his story. Her eyebrows went up when I got to Edward's financial assets disappearing.

"That's hard to read. The only person above suspicion for that would be Dillon himself, since he would be getting it anyway."

"I don't know where to go with that. The brokerage houses don't share information even when the assets don't go to offshore accounts. Anyway, Dillon wanted to hire us so I said OK. The deposit check he gave me is on the desk downstairs. Two thousand dollars."

"Good job. At least we're getting paid now, although there haven't been many bills."

"Executive salaries, winning auction bids, and so on. We can expense the Mazilu now that it's been stolen." This was followed by an unintended sigh.

"I feel like there's more," she said.

"You know how I told you I was going to ignore the Rocio parts of the journals and focus only on the Veronica."

She nodded silently. When I didn't go on, she did. "You were trying to be high-minded again. We've seen that before. That's so like you, but it doesn't work every time because then you always leave the practical stuff to Cody and me. Somebody has to do it when the high-minded people can't or won't."

I stared at her for a moment, looking for a subtext in that. "You're right. I don't think there's been anything high-minded from the killers in this case. I've been wasting my time, so now I've changed my mind about being high-minded."

"What made you decide that?"

"I wasn't getting anywhere other than a lot of classical and medieval allusions. I was feeling more erudite than effective. Edward must have thought himself a great scholar at times, maybe because he could paint in all those historic styles, but in the journals he seemed to be mostly stroking his own ego. I decided I was being foolish by segregating some of the entries out of a vague desire to give Rocio and Edward some privacy. The real stuff must lie elsewhere, beyond the limits of what I was reading."

"The heart of the message. How far have you gotten with that idea?"

I gave her a closer look, wondering from her tone whether her attitude wasn't a little more self-satisfied than curious, but I wasn't sure what that meant. "Only one entry about her being gone, and how cold the bed was."

"I'm sure. Winter was approaching when he disappeared. Was it getting any more interesting?"

"Marginally, if his moaning about her absence and getting all mystical about it is interesting. Anyway I did feel there was something more real in it. At least it was current. Edward writing alone about his research has the quality of a guy who finds himself at the micro-phone for the first time in front of a large crowd. You can't get him to sit down again."

"Like any Mexican official would be on every public occasion." After a moment, shifting gears, she added more. "So have you found those parts yet about how great her boobs were?"

Here her mastery of American slang again betrayed itself, but there was more than that going on. I also felt the balance shifting slightly away from my end

of the court, if it had ever been there, and I had to remind myself that Maya and I were always on the same
side in this business, mostly. The same side part was the
official policy, even if the reality differed from that now
and then.

"Ah, I did come across that idea early on, and I
quickly moved away, covering my eyes. But did I, by the
way, mention that to you? I don't recall saying anything
about it."

"You didn't have to." Here she lifted the journal
volume, flipped through it as if it was the most familiar
of territories, even boring at times, and set it back on the
table. My mental calculator was now spinning as if from
the input of bad data. Something occurred to me.

"You've read them too, but not the same pages as
I have," I said in a conciliatory tone.

"Yes, and you may have noticed that you only
tend to read one volume at a time."

Here I nodded as if I were a quick study, realizing
at the same time that quick studies rarely need to nod
when receiving new information. Although I had not
thought much about it, often when I picked up a journal
volume, the other one was not in view. There was no
reason Maya shouldn't have read them from cover to
cover. Or perhaps she only read those passages she knew
I was avoiding. I decided to fold my hand. The trump
cards were all in hers.

"So what have you discovered from reading the other passages? Tell me. You have the missing half of the data, and maybe we can now guess that's closer to eighty percent of the useful parts."

She nodded slowly. "Well, I know what Edward thought Rocio knew. Sometimes he must have been right, although I think he wasn't always because as time went on he was paying less and less attention to her. I wonder how well he saw her in the final two years. She's probably said something about that to you."

"More than once, and her book of poetry dealt with some of that. Maybe you saw it too."

She didn't address this. "Maybe you know more from talking to her than you are saying. I think you've discovered a certain kinship with her." Her eyebrows went up in a question mark.

"We're not cousins, and she doesn't ever weep on my shoulder. In fact, I haven't seen her shed tears about any of this. Anyway, I'm just an investigator."

Maya looked back at me with a degree or two of coolness for a while. "We talked before about Rocio sending Edward a subtle message toward the end."

"Yes. You thought there could be a tipping point in their relationship, one she set up. Truthfully, I wouldn't put it past her."

"There was. Edward walked in on her and Ray in bed."

Here I was unavoidably reminded of a scene in the case we filed as *Angel Face*, where I had quite innocently gazed over the third floor parapet of our house to observe Maya in the arms of another man in the garden below. The fact that he was an attractive monsignor of high rank in the Catholic Church had made that scene more disturbing, rather than less.

"And what was Edward's reaction to that discovery?" I said slowly, remembering my own in its precise degree of discomfort. I wondered if Maya had thought of that moment too when she brought it up. She must have. It was one of those unresolvable points in a relationship where you can either move on or not, but a clear solution was not available then or later. At the same time, I felt then it had happened more by chance than by choice, unlike the scene with Ray and Rocio. That had been a tipping point, a speed bump where she had laid in the curved pavers in advance on a stretch of road where he wouldn't expect them.

"Which one? In his narrative, Edward's first reaction was to murder Ray on the spot, as he said at the time while he looked around for a weapon. I'm surprised you missed that part. Or his next one, two minutes later, as he pulled himself together, which was to write Rocio off as his partner, which he told her not much later?"

"To me," I said, "that sounds like a failure of nerve. We know now that Ray outlived him by fifteen months or so. The part I would like to know is why Edward didn't choose that first option and kill Ray outright?"

Maya did not respond immediately. I already knew that Mexicans usually avoid conflict when they can, not from any kind of cowardice, but more from the absence of a way of dealing with confrontation in the structure of their manners. Had that also been Rocio's reaction? How could that work when Edward interrupted them? And what did Lebanese men do when caught in bed with the wrong person?

"I don't know why, because he didn't put in the detail of what happened. But before he could respond further, Rocio packed up and left. Women have some pride, you know, and Rocio perhaps has more than most women have, but not necessarily more than I do. He treated her like a dirty sock. Edward doesn't mention Ray again after that."

Entering this conversation a more personal element was creeping in, an implicit comparison between investigators and victims. I had seen this before. Sometimes the gap between those two points of view was not great enough to offer much comfort, and some cases could be like holding a mirror up to ourselves.

"Yes, Rocio Valdez would've had her pride, and her triumph as well." I said, thinking I could've taught a series of seminars on pride at the Instituto Allende, more focused on its manifestations than on its origins. For me, pride comes from what you do rather than how you define yourself, or from your class or family or background.

"How did that happen, when he caught them? He must have thought he trapped her, and she must've thought that as well about him."

"Well, Edward left on one of his trips, at least as he told her at the time. The journal doesn't offer his destination. Perhaps there was none. Rocio had already started to pack her own gear before he left. I saw that part too, because he also saw it right away. As the airport driver picked him up at five in the morning, he said a normal goodbye to her that they both knew without saying was final. She didn't know he was coming back, but she had been careless with Ray numerous times, knowing that one of them would work."

"She was intentionally careless, but he didn't say anything more about a confrontation?"

Maya shrugged. "Men don't fight duels over women anymore, not even here. What would you have done?"

As Maya said this, speculating to some degree, I realized that I hadn't felt Edward's pain before. Even in the single passage I read about Rocio's absence from their bed, it seemed abstract, almost self-consciously artistic in tone—and that would be his way of seeing it. He was sublimating her absence more than feeling it. But in

Maya's voice the tale had come alive.

In my limited scan of the journals I had come across none of this. In our three conversations, I felt Rocio had been frank with me in all of them, but frankness doesn't imply full revelation. It can be selective, and while I always tried to scan the nuance, hoping but not quite believing that subtle means complete, Edward still had his own take on the end of their relationship. That was the version I had chosen to ignore.

"Can you answer that?" Maya said with a slight tone of impatience.

"What?" I had lost the thread.

"What would you have done?"

I looked at her face for a long time, framed as she was between the beech wood uprights of the easel. Maybe I should use the newly stretched portrait canvas for her, just for a straight up head and shoulders. In our nearly nine years together she had changed in subtle ways, as I had. The challenge now was really seeing her as if I never had before, since I looked at her every day. That was something I knew I could do. And then, in the same moment, I had the answer to her repeated question. I stood up.

"I would've turned around and walked away without a word. I would've assumed you had made your choice, and any protest I might put up in that context wouldn't change it. But I would've also been surprised, because it would mean that you were either sloppy and uncaring about getting caught, or like Rocio, you thought that getting caught could provoke a decision that hadn't come under its own power. Neither one would be like you. You and I can still talk things through without needing to use tipping points like that."

She gave this a slow nod. "You're right. That's not my style. So why is it hers? You know her much better than Cody or I do."

"I think that was more about Edward than about Rocio. I know she had trouble getting his attention, and in one of our conversations she talked about Edward's contempt for reality. He simply didn't care about it. Maybe he's like a fiction writer. He lives in two different worlds and he can choose which one he prefers at any given moment."

"Now I understand about the Veronica better."

"Yes. None of this is about anything that's real."

"I was almost feeling bad for a while because the Church means nothing to me. I thought I couldn't understand this case because of that."

"I don't think it meant anything to Edward, either. But if you or I don't understand this, it won't be because of our lack of commitment to religion. Think of what he painted. He was a world-class forger, better, I'm sure, than the person who painted the version of the Veronica Edward was chasing. That's the real connection here. Edward wanted to own the *ultimate forgery*. I think if the artifact he found and hid in the back of the Mazilu had been what it pretended to be it would not have captured his lasting interest."

She looked at me for a moment. "That's where it was?"

"It had to be." I think at that point I needed to tell her something she hadn't found in the journals. At least she hadn't mentioned it if she had.

"Now I know why you used to be head of the Paul Zacher Agency."

"Yes! It was never just an accident of birth. Now that we've gotten through that, who was Edward Jericho? Have you gotten a sense of that?"

Maya nodded slowly. Given his journals as primary sources, I knew that her historian's mind would've approached them as a research opportunity far more than I had. While they were a crime story for me, for Maya they offered a study in character, always a challenge to a historian.

"Yes and no," she said. "But he made me think of my research on historical figures in the Mexican War of Independence. I think Edward was blank to himself. Without a brush in his hand, painting in the style of someone else, he couldn't have answered your question. The proper question to ask Edward was this: Who are you today?"

"Something you would say to an actor," I said.

"Exactly. His quests outside of painting were about pursuing something others thought was real, and if, like the Veronica, they weren't quite real to other people, they were still more real than he was to himself, because he gave their makers more authority than he granted to his own work. That's why he decided to hide it in the back of the Mazilu, if you're right. He didn't need to look at it again, because in finding it he was finished with that quest, and launched on the next one. What it really was didn't matter."

"And that conclusion," I said, "would've told him who he was? I have trouble seeing that."

"For that day, yes. But no, I don't think it ever did long term, that was only his continuing hope. That's not so different. Many people are defined by what they own, and then they go on to the next acquisition. Their stuff speaks for them and about them. Today's BMW says more about who they are than the three-year-old model they traded in for it. But I think Edward's process only told him who he might be next time. That was his constant chase, his *real* chase, even though it never worked."

"You're sounding like Cody now, but I suppose that's right. Where does that leave us?"

"That his values were very American in that way. It was still about what stuff he had to define him, even if that stuff wasn't a Mercedes or a grand house in Los

Balcones or Ojo de Agua."

This brought us further into some issues of
Cody and I being expats and the progressive change of
goals and values that comes with that status. We saw it
around us every day. This shed no more light on Edward,
however, and we adjourned to the loggia for a sunset
drink, thinking we had settled more small issues between
us than in the case of the Jericho journals. As the conversation tapered off we held hands as the sun went down
below the west wall.

CHAPTER NINETEEN

There's something that bothers me about those skeleton keys," Maya said, shaking her head at breakfast and pulling her hair off her face. "I was thinking about them when I woke up in the middle of the night. And you were snoring, by the way."

"I shouldn't have a glass of wine right before I go to bed, but it seems like we usually do."

"Delgado said you could buy them by the bucket for seventy-five pesos at the Tuesday Market. They're as cheap and as common as…"

"Hen's teeth," I said. She looked at me strangely as I took a sip of my coffee and bit into a slice of bacon. "Sure. His wife makes jewelry out of them."

"Hen's teeth? What could you make with…?"

"No, the keys that you find so troubling."

"Right, so why do we think because Ray had that key in his pocket that he put it there by his own?"

I gave her a look that signified a subtle breakthrough that I hadn't come up with myself, and in the same instant I also saw why. Unconscious assumptions are the bane of investigators. Once formed, they are as firm as concrete but nearly invisible, and always harder to spot than any physical evidence. The skeleton key in Ray's pocket was an example. Delgado fell for it too. In fact, he had sold it to us by the emphasis in his presentation, in the way he passed it around the table. Aha, he had said, in so many words, just look at this! But if someone had taken Ray's wallet and who knows what else from his pockets, why couldn't they have placed that key there too? Why would we think exchanges like that could go only in one direction?

"You're awfully clever for breakfast," I said. "I like that. My own synapses don't usually start to fire until about ten o'clock. And even then, it's only one at a time."

"I know. Thank you. That's why I'm the head of the Agency now."

"But I do think you're right, and now the message for us is this: What does Ray's killer want us to think by putting that key in his pocket? Messages like that go both ways. There is the obvious and the not so obvious. Often they're contradictory."

"The killer wants us to think that Ray was mainly focused on getting into Rocio's apartment, and after a brief search for the Veronica in the kitchen chair seats, then into her pants."

"Well, someone did some of that, at least," I said.

Maya nodded. "In spite of the footprints, I don't think it was Ray. This raises a question you brought up before. Why would Ray need to break in, when Rocio would have opened the door to him in some filmy negli-gée if she only had a little warning that he was coming? I can see you don't want to think she is so easy. But then, maybe you do?"

Maya could easily do more than one investiga-tion at once. "Nothing is that easy," I said. "Or, if it is, you'll always pay for it later. Easy usually only means deferred billing with no interest for ninety days."

A few minutes later I was clearing the breakfast dishes when something else came to me. Maya was still sitting at the table and hadn't finished her coffee. "It's funny how keys are like a motif in this case," I said. "It was those house keys in the kitchen that told Cody Edward hadn't left the property. Dillon brought that up to me again when he came by. Now this skeleton key, if it is planted, is supposed to tell Delgado something, and us, I suppose, too."

"You mean someone is sending us a message? But those keys in the kitchen made an awfully subtle clue, don't you think? How many people could get that?"

"Maybe, but the meaning is still quite clear if you take a moment to think about it. Not everyone would, and I missed it too."

"So did I, because we were both looking through

the auction lots and then paying for what we got. Cody was doing his usual snooping around. He thought something was hinky from right away. That's why you asked him to come. He wasn't distracted."

"It only needs one of us to notice what's going on," I said. As I wiped down the sink counter, Maya went up to change into her riding gear.

A key could be anything, not just a small profiled tool to open a lock. I had always thought the journals were the key to Edward's death, but if they were, I hadn't found the lock they would fit. And was the Mazilu painting the key to hiding the Veronica? Who had it now? I felt certain that whoever had it was the person who had killed Edward, and quite possibly Ray, unless Ray's death was only a copycat killing. But I didn't believe that. Everything about this case was too obscure to even decipher, not to mention copy.

I went up to the studio, this time finding both volumes of the journals, and started reading again with a different frame of reference. I suddenly felt the Jericho case was starting to wind down, but I couldn't have said why.

CHAPTER TWENTY
CODY WILLIAMS

C ody strolled down Prolongación Aldama from his third-floor condo late that same morning. Now, in early February, the weather had warmed, and planting season had officially begun on Candelaria, February 2, four days earlier. As he crossed the *jardín*, he nodded to a few expats he knew who were gathered on the cast iron benches to chat under the sculpted ficus trees with their designer coffees. He went on down to Mesones and turned left. Half a block farther on he paused before the entrance of Galeria Reflejo, which was on the same block anchored by the Angela Peralta Theater.

The gallery window offered passers-by a painting of two small Mexican children sitting on a wooden bench and eating *chorros*, the deep-fried bread sticks rolled in sugar. The colors were warm and lively, like those Paul would use, he thought, and Cody recognized it as a polished piece of work, although he was not a fan of smiling kids in paintings. He and his ex-wife had never had any children, and although he had saved two from drowning in his police career, it hadn't boosted his understanding of them. His wall at home boasted a LeRoy Neiman unsigned print of NFL football players clashing head to head on the field. As a piece of artwork it was a more accurate reflection of his former daily reality in the detective business.

He also understood just enough about painting from his conversations with Paul Zacher to realize he knew nothing about it. Even plausibly improvising on the subject was beyond him. The mere idea of soon talking about art with the gallery owner inside was making his mouth dry as he stood thinking about what to say when he walked in. Best to focus on the first picture he saw inside and try to bluff it, he thought. Say something about the drama of it, the impact on the eye. Paul often talked a lot about eyes.

Yet the issue of Edward Jericho's money disappearing had raised another question in his mind. What now remained of Edward's inventory of finished paintings, since none had been found in his home? And what was happening with the proceeds from the paintings that Galeria Reflejo had sold? Cody knew that neither Paul nor Maya had looked into this. While at first it hadn't seemed like a high priority, now was the time to check into it in more depth.

He stepped through the door with what he hoped was a confident look and closed it silently behind him. The atmosphere within was cool and somehow elegant, although it offered little embellishment. The walls were painted a pale putty green that seemed to push the artwork toward him in a subtle way, and picture lights hanging from a network of wires overhead accurately lit each piece. From somewhere deeper within, the sound system offered a mellow Spanish guitar tune. He felt himself relaxing, if only slightly.

When no one appeared, he moved forward toward a wall displaying three paintings that looked almost like landscapes, except that on closer inspection of the surface, nothing could be made out but paint. At that distance the illusion dissolved, and none of the shapes that had looked almost identifiable from fifteen feet away now made any sense at all. Nor did they show the marks of brushwork, but instead seemed thickly layered on with a flexible knife. He could see this from the way the edges stood up between strokes. Cody scratched his chin and stood upright, then took two steps back. Was this one a river scene, with a chunky meandering ribbon of highway nearby, and a few clusters of low slab-like buildings that displayed no doors or windows? The colors were pleasing enough together, all pastels and muted earth tones. They gave him a sense of harmony and reason, but not of any meaning, exactly. It made him ask himself whether he might be expecting the wrong thing. Should he be looking at these pictures differently? He recalled Paul being drawn into their first case for exactly that reason, that he might see things in a manner different from the way the police did. Maybe it was about the different ways people's eyes might be constructed, he thought, with his background in forensics, his faith in physical science. By this point he had completely forgotten about drama and the impact on the eye.

But for all that, he recognized that Paul, with his forthright commitment to the representational image, did not ever paint like this.

Cody advanced to the canvas again and slid on his reading glasses as he bent forward inches from the surface, scanning the detail. There, as he thought, he could see the actual canvas between paint layers! At some edges, the artist had allowed the weave to show through, tinted with only a trace of a beige primer. Somehow that worked, but Cody couldn't have said why or how. His first impression was that to leave the fabric showing must be a mistake, but he instantly understood that was not true.

"That's a great effect, isn't it?" said a voice from behind him. "I have two others in storage too, if you'd like to see them as well." A tall woman with dark hair stepped forward and offered her hand as he started upright. "My name is Claudia Preston."

She was dressed in a businesslike navy blue sheath dress with a belt and white trim at the collar and sleeves. Cody guessed her age to be about thirty-five. Her long dark hair was collected in a swirl at the top of her head.

"Are you the owner?"

"Yes."

"I'm Cody Williams."

"These three paintings are the work of Armando Pérez. He lives in Guadalajara. This series is called *Landscapes of the Mind*. Some critics describe them as psychological. I tend to agree, but not everyone does. What do you think?"

Cody, whose degree was in psychology, found nothing to respond to in this. He thought he might stutter if he tried. "I'm actually looking for something more, ah, traditional." Here his right hand moved uneasily from side to side, as if waving some obstruction out of his path, or displaying a new onset of palsy. "Like real people, that kind of thing. Work that maybe looks old, even if it isn't? I mean, when it's done in the old style, you know?" He smiled at her hopefully, not wanting to use the word *copy*. He had only ever seen one picture painted by Edward, and that was the Mazilu copy.

In her look he felt she had already sized him up as the art novice he was. He should've asked Paul to do this visit but he wanted to bring some new information to the case, since other than his house key insights at the auction and the rescue of Rocio, he hadn't had much more to offer. Part of the problem was that it was centered so much on art that he felt off balance and uninformed. Back in Peoria, the police force had been able to bring in consultants when required.

Claudia Preston hesitated for a moment. "I might have something like that. Please come this way."

Two freestanding partitions divided the gallery space into three equal areas. She led him to the far side of the second and they paused.

This has got to be Edward's work, Cody thought. "I like this style! Who painted these?"

"Well, the answer is now a bit sad, although not for the collector. It's a local artist named Edward Jericho. He died a little over a year ago, so his work has only been moving up in value since then. You understand how that works, right?"

He nodded vaguely. Possibly it was because the supply would never increase again.

The wall before them displayed three striking portraits of women. Cody realized that the precise detail of this painting style was a good fit with the Mazilu. The first to catch his eye was the image of a young reddish-blonde with a scarlet and gold circular hat, bearing a disdainful look, her eyes half-closed. She was dressed in an off-the-shoulder gown of a rich brocade fabric while she gripped a chain of pearls in her left hand as if it were

a bauble of no great value, only a prop that said something about her that Cody could not immediately read.

"Woof," he whispered, trying immediately to
cover this unintended comment with a sharp cough.

"Well, yes, I do believe 'woof' would be the
intended response in this case," said Claudia, casting him
an ironic sideways glance. "This is a copy of a painting by Frank Cadogan Cowper. That's the kind of thing
Edward likes to do, or did. The original is from about
1910, and of the school he liked to emulate most, the
Pre-Raphaelites."

Taking in this painting, Cody had a sudden flash
of insight about how it must've felt for Edward to be able
to portray an elegant woman like that, even if it was a
copy of an earlier work. Paul had obviously gotten into
it to the same degree. Clearly, there was more to this art
business than he realized. Even having Maya at his side
to view these paintings would've been a great help. As
she well knew, *woof* was often his response to her, too, and
she sometimes tried to speak for Paul on the subject of
art when he wasn't around.

"I'm also going to tell you something rather sad,"
he said to Claudia. He had prepared this as he walked
down the hill, rephrasing it now to make it sound more
spontaneous. "Although I didn't know Edward Jericho
personally, I attended his household auction at the end,
where I was surprised to see that none of his paintings

were available. I had hoped to get one of them then."

She nodded immediately. "I heard that too, that no paintings of his were offered. In a way I wasn't sad to hear that, though, since I would prefer to sell them from the gallery, but it did make me wonder where they had gone."

This told Cody nothing. "But do you understand why there were none at the auction? Because no other gallery here represented him, right?"

Claudia Preston frowned and she folded her arms. "No, we're the only one. And as far as I know, he didn't show anywhere else in México. Or anywhere, for that matter. Edward wasn't hugely productive and we were easily able to place everything he sent us."

"So these three here are the last of his that you'll ever have?"

"Well, I hope that's not true. There's always the possibility of a resale, or an estate consignment, but this one that you like so much came to us about two months ago. And we've received others too, since Edward disappeared. I mean paintings of his that we hadn't seen before."

"Two months ago? How does that work, if you don't mind me asking?"

"The consignor was always Edward's brother, Dillon. That didn't seem odd to me, with Edward off on one of his trips somewhere inaccessible, as we all thought.

Even when we found out that Edward was dead, it still seemed right that Dillon would've been the heir. Edward wasn't married and he didn't have any children. And Dillon did have the paintings. I guess that was the clincher for me. I always thought that in his absence Edward had arranged with Dillon to continue supplying us. That would only be good business."

"Did you ever see Dillon face to face in any of those transactions?"

"No. I've never met him. All his pictures came to us from a delivery service, even when Edward was still alive. That was not any different, whether he was in town or not."

"And did you communicate with Dillon directly?"

"No."

"When one was sold, where did you send the money?"

As Claudia Preston gave him a long, hesitant look she moved back a half step. "You didn't come here to buy a picture, did you, Mr. Williams?"

"No, I'm an investigator with the Paul Zacher Agency."

She nodded slowly. "I have heard of them. I suppose I shouldn't be surprised that they're involved in this."

"We were hired by Dillon to look into his brother's murder. I'm sorry if I led you on, because you've been very helpful. It's just that sometimes people are more willing to talk to me if they don't know why I need the information."

Her tone softened. "I do understand. It's a horrible situation. Anyway, to answer your question, I had always deposited his share of the money into an account of Edward's. If you had bought this painting today, that's what I would still do."

Cody gave her the name of the New Orleans bank where Edward kept his cash account. Dillon had furnished the Agency with copies of the statements.

"That's the one."

"Do you recall the name of the delivery service that brings these in for you?"

"No. It was always just someone with a truck, and rarely the same person, I think. At least I didn't recognize him from one visit to the next. And there were never any company names on the sides, not that I saw anyway. But if you live here, you know that's how business is usually done. The paintings were always securely wrapped, as if by someone that knew their value."

"Dillon never called to tell you one was coming?"

"No, it was only the delivery service that called ahead."

Cody looked back at the portrait. "How much does this one go for?"

"Six thousand, U.S. The original is in Melbourne.

It sold five years ago for about $420,000."

"I see. I guess I'll have to wait until I get promoted to chief investigator."

"Perhaps you could leave a deposit to hold it till then."

"Do you know Rocio Valdez?" He watched her reaction, but it gave him nothing unusual.

"I've met her here at a couple of openings, maybe more like five. I know that she and Edward were together for several years."

"The police think she may have killed Edward." This was an indirect way of asking her what she thought about Rocio's character. Cody was still trying to keep his tone unthreatening.

"I guess it could've been anyone." Claudia's tone was as cool as her face. "When you're in a relationship with someone, strange things can develop over time. I mean, I don't have anything against her, I've just never known her that well. Edward was what you'd have to call a 'special' sort of person. Not every woman would want to put up with him. I don't think I could've, even as talented as he was, and I'm a huge fan of good painting. Maybe that will tell you something more about her."

"And they always got along when you saw them together?"

"They were the kind of star couple that could bring in the press. I just loved it when they showed up!

Even though Rocio could be a bit reserved, she was still nothing but classy and photogenic, and gallery openings, even if they weren't for his own work, always put Edward on his best behavior. But behind that glittering opening night image, his reputation was that not many other things made him behave quite that well." Her eyes moved steadily back to the portrait as a small, silent pause hung between them.

"Would you like to say any more about that?" He looked equally as hard at the woman's face in the picture. Edward had certainly been a master at his trade, but Cody was now feeling that, with an unanticipated lurch, the case was in motion again.

Claudia turned and faced him with her hands on her hips. "I know that your own Paul Zacher is a painter, OK? Word gets around in this town, so I've also heard he has an eye for good-looking women, but that he's not a hell-raiser. In contrast, Edward Jericho was often a madman, in the old tradition of Toulouse Lautrec or Paul Gauguin. He could drink most of us under the table, and I don't know if you realize this, but you can still get absinthe here, the real brew made from wormwood that drives people crazy over time as it gets them loaded. That was Edward's favorite."

"You mean that if someone hadn't killed Edward, he would've…"

"Yes, he would've done it himself not too far

down the road. If you want to see that side of him, go ask around at the Casa Azul. It's a little dive of a music bar down off Calle Vergel, past the end of Pila Seca, named for Frida Kahlo's blue house in Mexico City. Not many people know about it, and I'm sure no tourist has ever found it, but they do know all about Edward there, and it won't be hard to find someone to talk about him. Please don't mention my name if you decide to stop in."

As Cody thanked her and said goodbye, Claudia Preston offered him her hand and gave him a wry smile as if she thought he might come back some day for one picture of Edward's in particular, the Cowper copy.

Outside on Calle Mesones the traffic was light. Cody found himself trying to imagine who might still possess an inventory of Edward's paintings. Surely Claudia had been mistaken; it was not Dillon. Wouldn't he have mentioned that to Paul when they talked about Edward's assets disappearing? Suppose Edward had been storing seven or eight paintings in the house, letting them dry before sending them to the gallery. Had his killer removed them and continued to ship them to Claudia Preston at intervals, maintaining the pretense of being Dillon? But if she always sent the payments to Edward's bank in New Orleans, what benefit would the killer find in that?

Perhaps it was the same person who had made off with all the assets, and he was merely waiting for more funds to pile up from picture sales to drain the accounts again. Greedy bastard, Cody thought, after getting away with a million and a half dollars already.

In the meantime, he and Paul would be scheduling a visit to Casa Azul.

CHAPTER TWENTY-ONE

At about lunchtime I was shopping at the Mega Market when Cody phoned me with a report on his visit to Galeria Reflejo. This was a surprise, since I knew that talking about art with anyone outside our circle always made him uncomfortable. The information that Edward's paintings were still coming into the gallery and the money from their sales was still being paid into his old bank account in New Orleans was also startling. Clearly we should've checked this out earlier. As a partial explanation for the ongoing supply, Cody thought that some of these pictures must have been drying during this time.

As for Edward needing to thoroughly dry his finished canvases for several months, as I did for my oils before I varnished them, that was not the case, and I told Cody so. Edward painted not in oils, but in acrylics, which dry overnight. If there was still a hoard of his work out there being fed to the gallery one or two pieces at a time, it wasn't for reasons of not being thoroughly dry.

In any case, after this much time, there would've been no question of any of his work still needing to dry, even if he had painted occasionally in oils. Still, like Cody, I didn't think Dillon was really behind this, but I had to be sure, so I dialed his cell.

He was back in the States, both surprised to hear from me and hopeful that my call meant more progress in the case. Perhaps I had given him the wrong idea of our degree of efficiency by telling him about the journals when the ink was barely dry on his check. When he picked up I was standing in the jalapeño pepper and bean aisle, just down from the salsas, bent over looking for the variety of whole black beans Maya favors. He got right to the point, which was startling, because that never happens here. You always get four or five rounds of greetings and family health queries first.

"Great to hear from you! What have you got for me today, Paul?" Nothing about the status of Maya and her horse or the Agency? The weather? How was my health or my mother's? I was thinking like a Mexican as I heard the sound of papers being shuffled as he cleared a space on his desk to receive my big news without any preamble. A lot of people here think Americans have no manners, and this lack of preliminary grace notes is the reason.

"Today I've got for you two sweaty corduroy jackets and a silk Tommy Bahama shirt with a ketchup stain on the pocket," I said, unable to restrain myself. "I'd like to pick them up Tuesday after lunch."

I located two cans of la Costeña black beans and set them in my cart next to the stack of baked corn tostada shells and three bottles of the Chilean red that Maya and I like to close our day with.

"Haha! Now you're breaking me up! Really though, Paul, you are *such* a kidder. You always know how to get me going." I didn't realize we went back that far. Even so, I detected a developing trace of impatience in his voice.

"I know I should ease up sometimes, but finding a little humor in these cases is what keeps me sane." It came to me suddenly that this conversation, for Dillon, was all about his brother's murder and he may not have seen any humor in it. "What I really have for you today is a question, not an answer or an outcome." I told him about Edward's paintings continuing to dribble into the gallery. Had they really come from Dillon? A long moment of silence followed.

"I suppose there's no doubt that they're really his, right? I mean, that he actually painted them?"

"Are you suggesting they might be the real paintings and not his copies?" I hadn't thought of this, and I wasn't sure how it could make any sense.

"Well, if he was such a great copyist, as you have told me a couple of times, couldn't that happen?"

"I just don't see that being the issue here, Dillon. This information came from Claudia Preston at the gallery where he showed, and she has looked at and sold more of Edward's work than anyone. I'm sure she would know. Although, as you suggest, I can't think of a better copyist of high-end paintings than Edward. I've done some of it myself and I would never put my own copies up against his."

This reminded me that I had done three wonderful Matisses in a case we filed as *The Theft of the Virgin*. What I liked most about them was that they weren't copies. I had gotten inside Matisse's head and invented those images as he would've done himself in the late 1930s. I understood the vocabulary of his style in that period. I didn't say to Dillon that this went far beyond what Edward was capable of. My buyer in Guadalajara had snapped them up, even knowing what they were. I always signed my own name to the back of efforts like that.

"Well, none of those pictures have ever come from me, if that's what she told you. I have never owned a painting by my brother, and I've never acted as a go-between for him and his gallery, either." I wondered if I detected a stuffy note of pride in his voice. "At this point, if I were you, I would be taking a hard look at that Preston woman too. Do you know what I mean? Maybe she knows who murdered Edward and she's disposing of the paintings for the killer just to have her cut. Or is she close to Rocio Valdez? Could it be that Rocio herself has some of Edward's pictures that she loaded into her pickup after she stabbed him? I'm so glad that you're on this, because maybe it's a much bigger story than any of us believed."

Or much smaller, I thought, without saying it. I struggled not to laugh over the image of Rocio Valdez cruising off in a pickup full of Edward's archival master-pieces. Why not put her in bib overalls and pigtails, too, as she drove away, bumping over the cobblestones, laugh-ing and chewing gum? I made a note to screen future clients a little better, just as I had on almost every prior case at some point not very different from this one.

"Haven't you noticed the picture money from Galleria Reflejo coming in payment by payment into Edward's bank account? Its probably not that often, only when a picture sells."

"Well, yes. The statements show it's happened five times, to be exact, since he vanished. In every case the money was transferred out again before I could get to it."

"You haven't been checking it online?"

"Well, no. But I can see it on the monthly state-ments when they arrive. Don't forget I do have some other businesses to run here."

"Have you thought about closing that account

and setting up a different way for Claudia Preston to remit the sale money?"

"I have thought about that, but it's not like this much money is the end of the world. It's usually two to four thousand dollars each time. I keep thinking I'll catch it coming in some time and divert it to my own account, just to see what the reaction out there might be, but it always seems to get past me."

"That's good to know." My estimate of his character and competence dropped by two-thirds. "Claudia Preston still has three of his paintings, so I will definitely keep you posted on this," I said, feeling equally as blunt as I turned my cart in the direction of the deli counter and said a friendly, but businesslike, goodbye.

Was there an element of not wanting to benefit from Edward's artistic output? Was his own money better than Edward's? Inheriting his brother's money from the bequest would've clearly been all right because of its volume. For the rest, it seemed like there was a more deeply rooted conflict here than I had yet seen, but then I wondered whether it could have any bearing on Edward's death.

While I ordered half a kilo of smoked turkey breast and waited for it to be sliced, I was also asking myself how sharp Dillon Gericault really was, and why was he so suspicious of both Rocio and Claudia? I couldn't help but recall Rocio's comments about how distant from ordinary reality Edward had been. Maybe Dillon carried that same maverick gene of disengagement, of rejection of the way things are, but it was still an attitude that formed a far better fit for an expat painter than for the owner of six dry cleaning establishments in a town where people easily spilled on themselves while celebrating.

Part of my assignment as a painter, especially of portraits, and in this Agency as well, is the question that asks how many ways there are for any of us to be. That matches the range of my skills in portraiture. How many of those ways would apply to Edward Jericho? Cody had added a few I didn't know about.

One item in Cody's verbal report I decided to give more weight to was Claudia Preston's tip about Casa Azul. To me, the way people entertain themselves rarely means much in a case, but that could also be the kind of oversight we always pay for later.

CHAPTER TWENTY-TWO

Casa Azul was the kind of place you'd walk past quickly if you were a tourist lost in an obscure neighborhood, especially in the late evening after taking a wrong turn. The chalky blue stucco was falling to the sidewalk in pie-sized pieces. The nearest streetlight was dim and hanging in its own lonely obscurity in the next block. Scanning the street where we stood I saw no window on the surrounding buildings, no matter how small, that was not heavily barred. Further down toward the intersection two dogs barked, calling to each other in a whiney tone that sounded more like desperation than hope. It would've been easier if Cody and I had wanted to talk to the proprietor and his guests earlier in the day, but we preferred to sample the atmosphere of the place in prime time. If that was about twenty minutes after midnight, we had gauged it right, since if this was where Edward had been hanging out to blow off steam, we'd soon hear about it. I couldn't imagine that Rocio Valdez had ever come here with him.

"Trust me on this one," Cody said. "The folks who planned to go home tonight are there already. The others, who may end up collapsing in the street, are only getting under way now. They're the ones we'll want to talk to, even if it is past my bedtime."

"Seems like we should've had a couple of tall ones to get ready for this," I said. "You know, to loosen us up. Won't they spot us now as aliens? Outsiders? Or worse, tourists?"

He shook his head as we approached the weathered door. "I don't think they'll notice us at all at this hour."

Inside, the lighting was economical. I could understand that. The three-tiered rate structure here encourages people to economize, and the dim effect enhanced the vagueness of the atmosphere. The long back wall was plastered with bullfight posters. These were all local, small in size, often with torn corners or other edge damage. They had clearly been harvested from walls and telephone poles after the bullfight was over, a process that would not leave many of them intact and collectible. Still, they continued to add some atmosphere in this sinister twilit zone.

To the patrons this display was only wallpaper. It provided ambiance, as they now did themselves. The conversation was a steady incoherent buzz, punctured by the occasional raucous laugh. My instinct was to look for painters, thinking of Claudia Preston's comment about Gauguin and Toulouse Lautrec's habits being mimicked here. It didn't matter that it was more than a hundred years later. At first I didn't see any artists I knew, although there was one table of four occupied by bikers in battered leather. Across the room I spotted a retired American anesthesiologist from Phoenix that I knew slightly, and he seemed confident that no one would recognize him here, so I quickly looked away. Slumped in his chair, he was deeply into the process of putting himself to sleep. It made me wonder if some doctors had a dark side. Why not? Too many of the rest of us do. As Claudia had told Cody, this tavern was where Edward had allowed his dark side to rule. Well, I thought, he had paid for it early in a way he hadn't imagined. Yet, hadn't there been that one remark late in the journals about how soon they would be coming for him?

Few people looked at us as we settled at one of the two remaining empty tables. Although we were neatly if not well dressed, there seemed to be no special dress code there. A small bandstand occupied the end of the room opposite the bar, but it was unoccupied except for three chairs and an empty mike stand. Flanking it on both sides were two violently abstract paintings, each about a meter square. They weren't bad if you wanted a lot of action on your walls, but it was more than I prefer on mine. Their style almost reminded me of the work of someone I knew, but I couldn't pull up the name. They made me wonder what Edward Jericho, with his fastidious Pre-Raphaelite technique, saw in this dive. Did it make him feel he was more connected to the heartbeat of some unsophisticated but genuinely Bohemian underworld? For me, that membership comes in some degree with every painter's brushstroke. Society is properly nervous about artists—they have come through the door uninvited and they mean to break a few rules before you have a chance to throw them out.

"So this is your kind of place?" Cody said. "At least they got some art on the walls here. But I wanna tell you, just from looking from table to table, this is the type of group where after closing I'd be going around collecting fingerprints from the glassware."

"Why do I think you learned something about art from your visit with Claudia Preston?"

"She does know the ropes. You couldn't talk to her without picking up a few tips, at least."

"Tell me what you learned from Edward's pictures at your gallery visit."

The waiter came by for our order, dressed in a grubby velour vest of a dark mahogany color he could've found at the Tuesday Market for twenty pesos. To his credit, Cody did not ask for his usual rum punch. He settled for a Bacardi Añejo on the rocks. I had a Stoli vodka. There is little that can be done to screw that up, and it's not so pricy that a place like Casa Azul wouldn't have it.

"I picked up a little insight about Edward Jericho," Cody said. "I think he was a fine painter, and looking at the three women's portraits they had, it made me understand you a bit better too. It's not just about painting nudes all the time."

"Right. The human body is only landscape. When I first started painting I was terrified of portraits, too, but my professor convinced me that the forms in the human face are no different from those you see when you walk through the countryside. They're all related. You just paint what you see without giving it a name. Words only get in your way."

I thought this was a simple and elegant way to sum it up. It was rare that Cody even tried to talk about art. As I waited serenely for his response, someone two tables away fell to the floor with a massive crash of glassware, and his chair skittered across the tiles. A few people glanced in that direction but no one got up except Cody and me. This told me something about the usual tone of Casa Azul; it was a deeply tolerant place.

When we reached him the man was squirming on his back without getting a grip on anything. One of the other people at his table placed a hand on Cody's elbow. "Let him be. He prefers to get up by himself. That way he can argue he's still sober. It's important to him."

Cody only nodded and we returned to our table, where the drinks had arrived.

"People can believe absolutely anything," I said. "And not only about themselves."

"I know. That's one of your core beliefs. That's also why we're in this business."

"See that guy second from the right end of the bar?" I said.

"I don't know him."

"It's Ernesto Gibbs," I said. "I just recognized him."

"The name is familiar."

"About ten or eleven cases back you were convinced he killed Victoria Mendez. You persuaded Delgado to bust him for it."

"That's right. I don't think I ever saw him before, though. He was that abstract painter."

"And those two paintings by the bandstand are his. Trust me, I know his work. It just took me a moment to remember who it was." He had long been known for his 'action paintings,' bold and vigorous abstractions reminiscent of the late forties and fifties. Later Gibbs had gone through a phase where he was using elements of Victoria Mendez's nude body as components on his canvases, the way you would use chips of colored stone in a mosaic. When she was murdered it wasn't hard to think he might have done it. Cody and Delgado were arguing he was obsessed with her. I agreed, but I never believed that meant he killed her. I thought it was rare for a creative person like a painter to be violent, much less a murderer.

Gibbs turned at that moment and caught my eye. Maybe his ears had been burning. I raised my hand and waved him over to our table.

Mixed Irish and Mexican parentage had given Gibbs a head of hair and a beard of darkest black. No conflict was evident in that blend, and little gray had made any headway with it. The hair was curly, and his barrel chest made him seem slightly top heavy as he approached. He wore a scruffy Cleveland Indians baseball cap with the brim turned backward, marked by half a dozen paint stains. It was a look that may have been too youthful for him, since he was in his mid fifties. When he reached our table after narrowly avoiding two others, he leaned over it with both palms flat on the scarred wood. He could've been holding it down in case a high wind moved through the place unexpectedly.

"Paul Zacher. I'll be damned if I haven't seen everything now. I can fuckin' die happy. What would bring a classy guy like you all the way down to a place like this?"

"Sit down," I said. "This is Cody. Cody, Ernesto Gibbs."

Cody reached out to shake his hand, but Ernesto

needed both of his own to keep steady. Then he sat down hard as if it was an unexpected decision.

"You're a painter, too," Cody said in a level tone, taking stock of him.

"I've been keeping that a secret, but I guess everything gets out in the end." He turned to me. "You got me out of jail that time."

"I never thought you killed Victoria. I just couldn't figure it."

"I cried for her in that jail, for that woman, when I was waiting for the hearing to get me out. She was never Vicki, you know, not to me, or anyone. I can still cry for her, sometimes. Maybe I will again tonight."

"I believe it. I saw some of the paintings you did with, let's say, elements of Victoria."

He shook his head. "What brings you in here now? Someone else get killed?"

I gave him a slow nod. "Edward Jericho."

"That's not news. But you must be tryin' to paint a picture of the crime."

"I'm trying to get to know him better so I can see who'd want to kill him."

"He was a little princess, I can tell you that. A little princess who was trying to kill himself. You could start with that. Eduardo, as we all called him, ought to be your *numero uno* suspect in his own death. You don't have to go any further. The man hated himself." Ernesto

273

stared down at the table surface as if there were something wrong with it.

"He was murdered by two deep stab wounds to the back," Cody said, eyeing his empty Bacardi glass with regret. "He must have had some help in dying."

"OK. One I could understand," Gibbs said. "But two says I'll have to agree with you."

"Can we buy you a drink?" I said. My own glass was empty. "Coffee?"

"I'll have what he's having." He pointed to Cody's glass.

I waved the waiter over and gave him the order. "So why would you say Edward hated himself?"

"Because when he wasn't painting like someone else he didn't have one damn clue in hell who he really was. Do you know about connoisseurs?" He leaned forward with a confidential look and moistened his lips with his tongue. Neither of us responded. "A connoisseur is a person who gets his status from his expertise about stuff other people have made. Paintings, like, for example. Eduardo thought that if he could paint as good as someone else, then he was as good as that person."

"Better," I said, "according to what one person who was close to him told me."

"There you are." The waiter set down the drinks.

"Did you like Edward's own painting style?" I said.

"Did he ever have one? Did I somehow miss it? You know how some people are nobodies? Edward Jericho was *everybody*. I think the only painter he couldn't mimic was me." He laughed coarsely. That was probably true, I thought.

"I saw a portrait he did of Rocio Valdez. He did a seamless graft of her head on another woman's body in a version of a painting by Lord Frederic Leighton. I thought it worked well, but it made me wonder why he didn't do more of his own work."

Studying his rum glass, Gibbs didn't respond.

"Why was he like that?" Cody said. "With all his skills I mean." His time with Claudia Preston had done him some good. He was now asking leading questions about art.

Gibbs placed his elbows on the table, leaving a broad space for the drink. "Don't want to sound too harsh, OK? But Eduardo had no soul. He must've been conceived by a couple of aliens who enjoyed the culture, but didn't have the knack to generate it by themselves. They were, however, copyists in possession of a brilliant gift." He lifted his glass and articulated the last sentence word by word as if he thought it ought to stay with us for a long time.

"And they passed it on to him," I said. "Do you know Rocio Valdez?"

"Not as much as I would like. Surely a real babe,

275

but I think she is not as warm as I would prefer in a woman. Speculating there, of course. All I can do."

Cody settled back into his chair, took a shallow swallow of his rum, then leaned forward with a confidential look. "Who killed Edward Jericho?"

"Cheers!" Gibbs held up his glass for a toast. "Love the intelligent questions. So different from this rowd. Crowd, I mean. You see that guy over there? He's the one that fell on the floor before. He's disgusting. But it was that feature exactly that Eduardo liked about this place. He wanted to hang with a rough crowd, as if that made him one of them."

"But you must've liked him, anyway," said Cody, drawing more deeply on his Bacardi Añejo again. I thought I could see an ironic curve to his lip as it followed the lower edge of his glass.

"Eduardo was a fuckin' wiener is what he was. Always pretending to be off looking for something too high class for anyone else to understand. That was that connoisseur thing I mentioned. You know how he would disappear for long stretches or maybe you don't."

"Sure," I said. "One of those, anyway."

"Ha! But what you don't know was that half the time when he was supposed to be off in Timbuktu or someplace, he was really right here, leading his absinthe lifestyle without his high falutin' poet girlfriend. I think she wasn't having any of it. She could probly use a touch

of coarseness herself, you know? I guess she's got the re-
finement part down all right, if you like that."

"Really!" said Cody, "You mean he wasn't actually in Timbuktu?" There was a curious chill in his voice,
one I had heard before in other situations. It came from
the draft he felt when a door was unexpectedly opening.
"I never thought of that. And did Edward stay somewhere around here then?" Inches above the table, his
index finger made a swirling motion to suggest the
immediate neighborhood, perhaps even this block.

"I s'pose you could say that. He had a studio right
around the corner. I was never up to see it, but it must've
been big enough to have a bed and a kitchen space. Usually when he left here he was in no shape to go very far
on his own."

"How did you know then about that space?" I
said.

"Well, old Eduardo was known to loosen up when
he drank, you know? Like a lot of people do." He made a
casual gesture that included everybody in the room. "He
told me about it one night. He had just come back from
his other place, his house, you know. He and Rocio had
some kind of blow up over her seeing another guy and I
sat down and talked to him after he'd had a few. He was a
sad case and sometimes I felt sorry for him, even though
he was a sap, OK?" Ernesto accompanied this with a
highly serious look.

"Was he staying alone there?" I said.

"I saw him with another Mexican woman a few times. Not a classy one like Rocio, but just kind of ordinary. Her name was Marcella and he said he found her out in the campo. She was like one that would keep the place up for him when he was gone, I 'spect. Wash his clothes when he threw up, but not so bright as Rocio. He needed a lot of taking care of."

"Do you know just where that studio was?" said Cody.

Gibbs shook is head. "Not exactly, but it was on the third floor somewhere. Not too many of those, right?"

CHAPTER TWENTY-THREE

ody and I had a similar thought as we left Casa Azul and walked toward my house on Quebrada, where he had parked. It was not far away. We were thinking that the second studio might be the source of Edward's later paintings that continued to trickle onto the market through Claudia Preston's gallery. Someone had probably been paying the rent as a place to store them, which couldn't have been much in that neighborhood, and kept it going as it had been at Edward's death.

"I think it's someone from that Eye of Horus group," Cody said. "Maybe there's a rivalry inside it, a lethal competition as they search for the Veronica, and one of them killed Ray as he got close to it. Maybe it was even Ray that switched your Mazilu and his killer has it now. Didn't Rigoberta say the man had a pirate beard? Ray certainly had that."

"Maybe they all did. Anyway, I think the Veronica is a foul thing. It was never genuine to begin with.

Didn't Edward say in the journal that thirty-some people have died trying to get it, or to hold on to it?"

"Maybe they're all connoisseurs," Cody said. "I thought that analysis Gibbs offered was very interesting, even if he was a bit loaded. It was obviously not the first time he'd thought about it. That you gain merit by the level of knowledge you have about valuable objects. It rubs off on you personally. Even if you can't do wonderful things yourself, you at least can recognize them better than other people can. It puts you in a certain class."

"So if you're an expert on the subtle nuances of garbage, it's not the same effect."

"Right. And Rocio must've had a role in that, too, in Edward's connoisseurship."

"Because she's a poet and an elegant woman," I said, "an embellishment and an ornament on the successful painter's arm. He was often seen with her around town. I wonder if that was the main point of their relationship." I paused on the stone curb, wondering if she had ever known who she was in bed with. Was he different people there too? But I could never ask her that.

"Her function was mainly decorative. So why would she put up with that? She must have been smart enough to see it. Even if not right away, she certainly did later."

"Was being with Edward flattering to her at the point in her career where it began? Poets have a hard time getting recognized. He was more established than she was. As a painter, you must have to think about promotion all the time."

We paused in silence while the well-used carcass of a 40-year-old muscle car bumped over the cobblestones with a subwoofer blaring that could've awakened everyone on the block.

"There are times when I wish I had a hearing aid to turn down," Cody said, "but nature has blessed me with good ears."

"I don't have to remind you that there have not been that many suspects in this case. One of them is dead. Dillon has pinned Rocio as his perpetrator, with Claudia Preston as co-conspirator, but I feel there must be a whole group of possible killers out there we've overlooked."

"Probably. But for Dillon," Cody said, "this has always been a women's conspiracy. I couldn't tell you why. In my experience, women make good friends and valuable allies and lovers, but they're rarely cooperating killers on their own. They can be formidable in business, but gangs of wild women did not terrorize the old West, OK? They did not ride in and shoot up Main Street. Nor were they hanged in great numbers for their crimes. Dillon's views are no more than long distance speculation. New Orleans gives him no standing in this town. He has no boots on the ground in this case, which makes all the difference."

I thought about this as Cody climbed into his small Ford and drove away. Edward may have had no boots on the ground here either, or in any other place. Nearly a year and a half after his death, whatever footprints he'd had anywhere were rapidly fading away, much like Ray's wet ones on the sidewalk outside Rocio's house.

At eleven the following morning, Cody and I met again at Casa Azul, not to relive a life-changing experience, or to inaugurate a more Bohemian lifestyle, or to have an early drink, but because we wanted to inspect the second Jericho studio in its current state, if we could find it.

Wherever else Ernesto Gibbs' alcohol induced vagueness had led him, he was clear on the idea that the studio must be nearby, since Edward's range of motion in the late evenings was often severely diminished.

It was a bright morning, warming as we circled the unpromising block that held Casa Azul. Our only clue was that the studio had been on the third floor of one of these buildings. Seeing nothing, we radiated outward from the corners. After ten minutes we had only seen three unpromising third story segments when a fourth appeared. We stepped back into the street to size it up, as we had done with each of the others.

The building was U-shaped in plan, with an opening at the sidewalk guarded by a pair of rust-finish steel doors. Several large scrubbed patches suggested the graffiti removal team's efforts. The entrance would be large enough to accommodate the passage of a medium sized truck. Only the left segment of the building was three stories high.

The wall next to the gates was blank on the first floor except for a steel door. Both levels above presented only a single window. Cody walked up to the door and scanned the frame. It offered no doorbell. Usually they're located at about head height to keep them out of the reach of children.

"What do you think?"

I shrugged. We went back out into the street and surveyed the rear of the third floor segment. The main level was out of sight behind the pair of tall doors, but the next two stories each had a walkway across the width of the building. The uppermost level had two doors and two windows facing that parking area. It couldn't have been a courtyard garden. Cody pointed toward the roofline.

"See that steel bar projecting about a meter past the walkway at the top?"

"Right."

"Just under the overhang it has a hand winch. I can see the crank for winding it, and the end of the bar has a hook. I can't make it out from here, but there must be a steel cable running between the two of them. What does that mean to you?"

"Possibly there's a narrow staircase inside, so this is a way of bringing larger or heavier things up."

"Edward Jericho could've lowered a large canvas down that way, or brought a blank one up if someone else was stretching his canvases for him. Did he ever paint big?"

"I guess. He certainly copied people who painted big. I haven't seen more than about twenty pictures of his, so Claudia Preston could answer that better than I could. But you know what? That winch also could've been used to lower Ray's body into the back of a car or pickup. Suppose Ray had caught up with the person who had the Veronica and got himself killed the same way Edward did?"

We had both brought our guns. "Knock first or pick the lock without messing around?" he said, pulling out his pocket tool kit.

"Just get us inside. If we see someone we can say we were out picking locks for practice and we did this one by mistake, not realizing anyone was at home." It's always easier to apologize here than to ask permission.

No cars were in view, or pedestrians. I kept watch while Cody got us through the door in about two minutes. Inside, the narrow enclosed stairway hugged the outside wall, lit by the single window over the second floor landing above. At that level a corridor ran toward the back with a single door on it. We took the next flight up to the third floor, where we paused to listen.

The building had a low-grade industrial feel, as if it had been adapted for cottage industries or a sweatshop. The walls were nubby plaster that had been painted in a light color long ago but now mainly bore the scuffmarks of years of traffic. They were slightly sticky in spots. In the center of the corridor, near the apartment door, hung a single bluish spiral bulb that reminded me of the ones in the morgue. The ambience inspired no sense of the Bohemian artist's life; it offered only dreariness. At the far end a door with a glass panel in the upper half led out to the walkway.

When we advanced silently over the tile to the apartment door I put my ear to it, but heard nothing. Again, the question was whether to knock or not, but if this was the guy who had murdered Edward and Ray, now wholesaling the stock of paintings Edward left behind, why give him any warning? If he had one, he could just fire his gun through the door.

I switched the .38 to my left hand and put my fingers on the knob. To my surprise, it turned silently. I pushed the door open a crack, watching the light form a strip along the jamb: still no sound. Cody was directly behind me as I opened it further. We were facing a short, half-lit hallway that ended in a blank wall about five meters on, where a passage led away on each side. On my left a door opened into a bedroom that held a neatly made double bed and a window that faced the street at the front of the building. Another door near the bed led into a bathroom. On the right was the entrance to the kitchen, which had a pair of windows that gave onto the back parking area. A smell of bacon hung on the air and a collection of freshly washed breakfast dishes dripped in the drainer by the sink. No one was in sight and there was still no sound. But if no one was at home, why was the entry door not locked?

Silently we continued down the hallway to the end. At the left, the opening led to a living room that fronted the street, and on the right to a small sitting area without windows. That was the one we chose. As I turned the corner I could see it was mainly a wall of storage cabinets similar to what I had in my studio, with a computer desk and a reading lamp in the far corner. At that point I froze in mid step.

Hanging over the desk was the Mazilu painting of the *Madonna in a Venetian Costume*. My Mazilu, but it lacked a frame. Because of our situation, I could not have uttered a sound, but I was already speechless anyway. Cody only shook his head and placed his fingers over his lips. At the opposite side of the room a wide archway, the only source of light, led to what must have once been Edward's low rent studio. The only good light was on the longer sides, at the street and at the parking area, and the far wall was blank red brick. From somewhere in the distance came a soft tapping, metal on metal, as if someone was pounding out a dent in a copper vessel. Or marking time.

Near the parking court side of the studio an easel stood with its back to us at a slight angle. I had the sense of movement on the other side, screened by a board or a panel. Through the uprights, I thought I saw feet at the base. We moved toward it silently, guns drawn. My ears were suddenly ringing.

Perhaps that was why I didn't hear us make any noise, but suddenly on the other side of the easel a person stood up with no warning. His hair and beard were matted and wild, black streaked with gray. My first thought was of the tattoo he must have on the back of his neck. Cody and I had been right in our speculations; there were more them. The man's look was almost crazed. I didn't recognize him until he spoke in a raspy voice.

"Paul Zacher! You? Have you come to kill me again? Are you one of them now?"

"Edward." My voice cracked.

Cody said, "What!"

This far into his murder case I could hardly speak Edward's name. I heard the sadness in my tone, in that single word, as I suddenly saw everything. He was wearing the same style of blue lab coat he always wore painting.

It took a long moment before I could speak again. "What happened to you?" Of course, I didn't see everything, only enough to overturn all of what I thought we'd learned about this case. He laughed bitterly.

"They came for me, as I knew they would, eventually. I had asked too many questions. I already had the Veronica by then. I hadn't considered what it would take to keep it, but I was able to kill the first one that came after me. He bent over it and I plunged a knife into his back. Then again. He had that strange tattoo, you see?" He leaned over and set down his brush.

"Who are they?" said Cody.

"Who are you?" Edward looked at him for the first time.

Like a comic moment in the heart of a deepening tragedy, I introduced them.

"It's a group from Lebanon. They're iconoclastic Christians; I can't pronounce their name, but it means Eye of Horus in medieval Arabic. They allow no images, and they have made it their mission to destroy the great iconic representations of Christ. I wasn't aware of them until I discovered how Irena Karski died in Cuernavaca, but the Veronica has long been their biggest target. They would simply destroy it."

"And destroy anyone who had it." My voice was almost a whisper. Uneasily, I realized that Cody and I were both standing there with our guns still hanging in our hands, pointing at the floor, but even so, at least somewhat ready. Edward's status was unclear now that we knew the truth, as was ours.

"What happened to Ray?" Cody said in the calmest of tones.

I could see the smile through Edward's beard. "Well, I had a small score to settle with Ray even before he realized it wasn't me in the ground at the house on Baeza. Let me say that Ray found me here, just as you did. I was ready for him, too, because I knew they would keep on coming."

"After all that, I can imagine you're always prepared now," I said. I had already heard the subtle movement behind us. It was not close, not yet. Possibly someone was just emerging from the office area at the far side of the studio. At the edge of my vision I saw a steely look creep over Cody's face, led by a tense line of muscle formed like a thin steel bar along his jaw.

"My dear friend Marcella is now behind both of you. As she approaches you will need to give her your guns, one at a time. You first, Paul. She has a very big .45 automatic that once belonged to my grandfather in his Army days." He gestured her forward. Edward's voice was as smooth and polished as if he had rehearsed this exact line for this precise moment. We might as well have had the Eye of Horus tattoos on our necks, I thought.

"Drop and shoot, *now*," said Cody in a hiss from the side of his mouth.

No thought was required. We both hit the floor at the same instant, but since this move was both un-rehearsed and unexpected, we had turned toward each other, and somehow there was a confusion of arms and legs for a half a second. The woman running toward us fired twice, and we each fired twice, all in about the same three seconds. She ran back into the office uninjured. I knew I wasn't hit, either. Cody was already getting up, shaking his head to clear it. The cluster of shots still rang in the air. Edward was not in view. The sharp smell of the explosive surrounded us. For a moment, with my gun aimed at the office archway, I waited for Marcella to re-turn, but she did not.

I walked around to the front of the easel. Edward was lying sprawled backward on the tile floor, bleeding heavily from his abdomen, with another stream coming from the right side of his body. Part of his blue lab jack-et was submerged in his blood. Cody elbowed past me and bent over him. I watched for a long moment as he touched Edward's wrist, neck, and chest.

"His vitals are very faint. I think he's going fast."

By then I had already turned away, dialing first for an ambulance and then Delgado. As I slid the phone back into my pocket, the tapping outside stopped. Edward's hairy face was ashen, his mouth moving slightly, opening and closing almost like that of a small fish. His eyes were vague and filmy. Death had already taken him by the hand and was leading him from the room.

Unable to watch this, I turned back to the easel to examine what Edward had been working on. I didn't want to think of him passing before someone could get there. Maybe Cody could somehow keep him alive, but it didn't look like it. In my mind I could only see Edward as he had been on Baeza, smooth, well groomed, the polished painter of genteel images from a different time. For all of us, he had been an escort to a different era and sensibility, as he had for himself. Rocio had said how little he cared for reality. Above all Edward would not have cared for this.

A sheet of Masonite about thirty-six by forty-eight inches rested on the bar of the easel. On it, two pieces of fabric of the same size were affixed with art gum or something like it that would not leave a trace or a pinhole. One image was the legendary Veronica. As I stared at it I found that it did not move me at all. The last act of the drama on the floor behind me was far more real.

The patina of the iconic piece was evident, and the wear marks and stains on the ancient filmy material were clear. The fabric of the other portrait next to it was nearly, but not quite, the same ultrafine texture, and obviously lighter in tone. Edward should have washed it in tea first. On the older version, the face of Christ was a near-perfect reproduction of a crude early charmless image of a kind that must have once graced simple churches all over Europe, the Middle East, and North Africa. Oddly dark in the skin tones, the mouth was weak and fitfully defined, and the eyes unfocused. Overall it had a two dimensional feel. Edward's nearly perfect copy was almost complete but for some details of the hair and on the crown of thorns. Still, the character of both pieces said nothing about the man behind the image—there had never been a model for it. It lacked any sense of a real presence, and that was what this case was all about, I thought.

But in addition to the two rectangular pieces of fabric there were two bullet holes in the board, one between the Veronicas, each as false as the other. The other hole was just below the older one. I realized that in this analytic study of the two, I was avoiding Edward's death. Had he been killed by irony? We had arrived intending to capture his killer and in so doing, set up his death.

"He's gone, Paul, now he's really gone," said Cody, getting to his feet and shaking his head. "That's all. They couldn't have saved him even if they'd gotten here when you called."

Feeling prepared for none of this, I felt my face puckering and my mouth tighten. I was able to add nothing as I turned to look at the body on the floor. Edward's eyes were almost closed. Any further closure would come from someone else now. He seemed much smaller than when he had stood up only five or six minutes ago and called my name. Although he was no one's idea of a great artist or a wonderful man, any person's death is still a tragedy. The last day of an artist is even worse for me. We're all difficult people, but that's because of the endlessly challenging nature of the territory we work. It offers too many opportunities to stumble, and sometimes we can't get up again. Edward, from this maze of obscure choices, had picked one of the more difficult ones.

I wished Maya had been there at that moment. The truth be told, I needed someone to lead me out of that room and put me into the passenger seat of the car, buckling my seatbelt for me while my hands were folded on my lap. I could do no more than stare blankly out the windshield. The end was no more profound than that. I really didn't care what had happened with Marcella. She'd made her best effort, thinking I suppose, to save Edward, and it didn't work, but neither had ours. She had been alert, she'd been armed, but she'd had no training for a situation like this. To shoot at us with Edward behind us was worse than naïve. She'd been neither smart nor creative enough to improvise in a complicated situation. I tried not to see the outcome as inevitable, but

I couldn't. Delgado could work out her fate; I was ready to go off duty. Cody's aging face seemed as bleak as I felt. I had to wonder when any of us had last looked like heroes. I couldn't recall.

Sitting at the easel I picked up Edward's tiny exquisite sable brush and wiped it free of the dark pigment of thorns and harsh shadows, before swirling it in a waiting cup of water to clean it. Then I carefully patted it dry before setting it bristles up in a ceramic brush vase next to his palette. It brought a single particle of order into a scene that offered no other.

Because I hadn't been able to give him the address, it took Diego Delgado thirty-five minutes to find us. During this time I was sitting out on the third-floor walkway, staring up at the hand winch, imagining Edward in darkness cranking Ray's dead body away on the end of a hooked cable, dropping notch by notch down to the service courtyard below. At least when Delgado arrived, the now useless ambulance crew was right behind him on the stairs. By that time I had lost my taste for the customary pleasantries.

As Delgado recorded the story from Cody I glanced around the studio. Hanging on the wall near the windows was a female nude I hadn't noticed, and I walked over to examine it more closely. Although I had glimpsed her face only for an instant was we exchanged bullets, I could see it was Marcella. A squat figure, she sat on a varnished wooden chair, leaning slightly forward. One hand rested carefully between her thighs. Her face was unappealing and her manner suggested she was less than half willing to pose in that fashion.

Worse, neither the chair nor the figure sat comfortably within the frame. They expressed a disturbing tension, not provocative, but merely an absence of balance. A visually discordant image, the elements were not at all right together, and the painting therefore lacked any sense of composition. Its assembled parts made less than a whole. When Edward had painted Rocio's head into the Frederic Leighton picture, it worked perfectly. But then, he'd had all of Leighton's cues and his flawless visual vocabulary in place as his starting point. Here, in a work that was only his own, Edward had failed in a larger sense, even though the detail and the brushwork were impeccable. I could only conclude that he had been a painter, but being an artist was beyond him. The Bohemian, absinthe-addled lifestyle could not change that, nor could the connoisseurship he cultivated make him appear the genius he wanted so much to be.

I turned to find Cody standing next to me. "A sad case," he said. "I think Edward Jericho tried to do too much. Why be chasing all those high-end pictures? Couldn't he just be a painter? I think you've got it right."

Later I exchanged a few words with Delgado, but

I had little to add to what Cody had already told him. He sensed my distress and treated me gently. I knew there would be another meeting at his office downtown once the body had been removed and Delgado had time to sort through the forensic aspects of the scene.

Knowing that Marcella's .45 had killed Edward, we gave Delgado our guns to check against the fatal bullets and said our goodbyes with the sense that while the case was not over, our involvement in it was.

Going out, I paused for a moment in the office. The forensic crew was still occupied back in the studio. Having the odd thought that they would find my fingerprints on Edward's sable brush, I plucked the Mazilu off the wall in a single gesture and carried it out with me. So who had taken it from my house? It could only have been Edward himself, since Ray was still looking for it when Edward killed him. Outside the door I turned the painting over, and found that the paper backing that had once hidden the Veronica was gone.

Farther out in the street I held the Mazilu edge on into the better light. There were no subtle paint ridges in this version. I had the feeling that the painting in my hands was one of the few genuine artifacts in this entire case.

I turned to find Cody at my side. "Poor Edward," he said.

"Indeed. Poor Edward."

CONCLUSION

It was good that the following week was a busy one, because it was easier to keep from ruminating too much about the sad end of Edward Jericho. Dillon flew back to San Miguel to settle Edward's estate for the second time. Among the papers in the small office next to the studio he discovered the brokerage statements for an offshore account that now held Edward's fortune, including the deposits from the more recent sales at Galeria Reflejo. He discovered five finished paintings leaning against the wall on a shadowy side of the studio. If he noticed the empty picture hanger on the wall over the office desk, he didn't mention it. Maya and Cody briefed him on the final days of Edward's life, gave him a reasonably realistic account of his death, and together they closed out the case in a meeting I did not attend. Once again, Dillon wrote a check, not a large one, with a smile on his face.

Within forty-eight hours of Edward's passing, Marcella was discovered and apprehended at the home of a cousin with a different last name who lived slightly out of town on the Cieneguita road. Delgado told me she had not yet been charged, although when she was, it might only be with accidental death, or even with discharging an illegal firearm, since she had not intended to kill Edward. She had only wished to kill Cody and me, and since we had not even been hit, well, the law was not too deeply offended. Justice here can be awfully literal-minded.

The anonymous ashes interred in Edward's niche at the Panteón were claimed by Delgado to be held for some future investigation during a slow period. Alone on a warmer day late in February Dillon supervised the installation of his brother's real ashes. It must have been an oddly moving but still ironic moment for this unlikely twin. I was happy to not attend a second memorial. I hung the real Mazilu back in my studio in its original frame, and sent Edward's copy by messenger to Dillon's hotel with a note saying it was time he finally had a finished example of Edward's work.

I found I couldn't speculate on what he might do with the awkward nude of Marcella. He could hardly fail to recognize what a difficult painting it was. I also didn't think the almost completed copy of the Veronica counted for anything, and it might have been returned to Dillon in a box with some other effects. I was not eager to see him again, although he had claimed he appreciated my sense of humor.

It wasn't much later that I ran into Rocio Valdez in the *jardín*, a place where sooner or later you will run into everyone in San Miguel. In the hug we traded I could feel something tentative on her side, a bit of tension as if she didn't know where we stood now after all that had happened. We exchanged the usual greetings and after that, from arm's length she looked deeply into my eyes.

I found I was in the mood to wrap things up, and Rocio seemed like the perfect person to do it with. On impulse I linked arms with her and we walked in a comfortable silence down Reloj to a small coffee shop I knew where we found an obscure table in the back. It fronted a tiny immaculate garden full of succulents in sculptural clay pots. We took the only table in the shade. The other two remained empty. We had placed our orders coming in. As we sat down, somewhere atop the walls a bird was singing its own unique song, but I couldn't see him.

"I knew you would find more to talk about, Paul," Rocio said. "I told you that after the memorial."

I couldn't help but smile. Maya would've enjoyed that introduction. "I'm trying to wrap up Edward's case in my own mind. There are some loose ends, a few things I still want to think about."

"Life is full of loose ends. They only multiply in our final days, and then they escape from our hands entirely, like releasing a flock of small birds." She demonstrated this.

"Then here is one of them, since we all come to a bad end. Were you surprised when you heard that Edward wasn't dead?"

She sighed and paused for a moment. "Well, when I heard about it he already was again. But initially I was, Paul, very much, but the longer I thought about it since, it began to make sense. That was only part of Edward's unreality. Why shouldn't his exit be a sham too? Even his staged death was a copy of someone else's, an intruder he had killed. As for my reaction now that he's really gone, I feel I had already done the grieving for him. And, having let everyone mourn his loss when he wasn't really lost, he doesn't deserve any more from me or the rest of us. We had already said our real goodbyes."

"And we all meant it. I know I did. Maybe that sounds cynical coming from me, the way it worked out."

"You didn't know him as well as I did, but no, that doesn't seem cynical. I think your position is not the easiest one to be in. You must be conflicted sometimes when your client turns out to be a criminal."

"That's happened several times. In the Agency we try to avoid turning people in to the law directly, although sometimes we do set it up. It depends on what they've hired us to do. We like to meet our obligations to them first."

"And Edward wasn't your client, not ever. Now you can be totally loyal to Dillon." Without laughing, she gave me an ironic smile, as if that would be an unlikely outcome.

"Who, by the way, believed you killed Edward." I tossed this off lightly, but I had heard plenty about her from Dillon, so maybe now she could give me her take on him.

She shook her head. "He never liked me, never even liked the idea of me. He was always the dry cleaner king and I was the poet. I was only one more way for the refined and artsy Edward to be superior to him."

This reminded me of something Ernesto Gibbs might say. The server came in with our coffee.

"This is my treat," Rocio said, touching my hand briefly.

"Thank you. I feel like I have to send the journals off to Dillon, since he's the heir, even though I won them at the auction. Do you have any objection to that?"

"No. It's so over now that Edward's died twice," Rocio said. "Those journals are dead too. They should've been cremated with him. And how odd that Dillon now has the Veronica! Could you ever have guessed it would end that way?"

"If he can hold on to it. I think it's an albatross, a bringer of misfortune and death. How much of the story of Edward's last days do you know?"

"Licenciado Delgado was kind enough to call me and tell me about the end and the way he was living since he disappeared. He also said that his girlfriend Marcella killed him accidentally." She did not appear to wish to get any more detail from me. I was OK with that; my role in it had left me with a queasy feeling. In the days since those last chaotic moments in Edward's studio, I had hardly stopped rethinking our actions. It always led nowhere.

"Maybe Dillon will want to tell this story some day, once he's read Edward's journals," I said, ready to move on.

"I think no one could tell it like you could."

I shrugged, thinking of Maya's greater probe of their relationship. "I'm only glad he decided not to have a second service for Edward. No one would've come. I've already written up the case file, since that's all I ever do, but I always do it immediately, while it's still fresh. One question I try to answer in every one of these case reports is this: Who was the victim, really? I feel I owe them that for the record, even though no one ever reads the reports but us. Not just the name, address, and the usual data. I had to leave anything beyond that blank this time, because I depend on my own conclusions to give the answer. You can see how I don't have an answer for how to characterize Edward." I didn't want to mention his limited skill as a painter or the inept unbalanced nude of Marcella, and my reaction to it. I didn't know whether Delgado had mentioned Marcella to her.

"I was telling the truth," Rocio said, "when I said I never looked into those journals, although I did know where he kept them. At the time when I said that I wondered whether you believed me."

"I wasn't sure what to think. I wanted to believe you, but I didn't see how you could resist reading some of them at least."

Her voice dropped to a whisper. "I didn't think Edward would be telling the truth, even in a highly personal record like that. I believe that especially now, but more than anything, that was what kept me from looking into them when I discovered where he hid them. Avoiding them was a sounder instinct than I ever realized at the time."

"Still, if you want to see them, I'll loan them to you before I send them on to Dillon."

Rocio only shook her head and again leaned toward me over the coffee cups.

"No, thank you. It's over," she said. "Just send them away to their next fictional setting in this story. Still, one thing puzzles me—the range of behavior Edward was capable of. I'll never understand it. He was the ultimate Pre-Raphaelite copyist, and then he was the boorish degenerate in his hovel, letting himself go to the point where he was scarcely recognizable. I suppose part of it must be the absinthe."

"In my Agency job I've learned that opposites can coexist. Think of the land of the midnight sun. Six months later, on the far side of its cycle, it becomes the land of darkness at noon. That's where Edward was, toward the end."

We said nothing more for a while. She stirred her coffee. In his journals Edward had voiced a variety of opinions about her, as had Diego Delgado, Maya, Dillon, and Ernesto Gibbs. I had taken my own impressions of Rocio Valdez without feeling that I knew her in any depth. I decided to push on anyway.

"In several passages Edward wrote how much he regretted your refusal pose nude for him. I wasn't looking for items like that; they only jumped out at me. I realize there are a lot of ways to understand why you wouldn't care to. I put it down to simple modesty, which requires no explanation."

"I would have, though, if he'd asked me early on. Later, two years into it, when he did ask me, I felt too vulnerable to do it. I would've wondered what he was seeing, looking at me like that." She shook her head.

"For Edward, that was a major lost opportunity. He did so little of his own work, his own vision." In spite of the inept Marcella painting, I found I could still believe that Rocio might have inspired him to a breakthrough effort. I stared at her for a long moment, wondering what kind of vulnerability she had felt that held her back. There was a period several years ago when I had painted a lot of nudes, and I always took care to make the model comfortable. That was basic to the process to both of us, since I can't paint a sense of grace and relaxation that isn't really there.

"I would pose for you, though, Paul. I know I could." She gave me a steady look that held nothing provocative.

"Then imagine us in the studio and I'm looking at you from behind the easel. What am I seeing that would be different from what Edward would've seen?"

"Hills and valleys, and the occasional outcropping of bush. I heard you say that once at a party Edward and I gave, and I've never forgotten it. But you would not see in my face the baggage from Edward that had already accumulated in our relationship by that time, because now it's gone."

Feedback from readers is important, both in telling the author what he's doing right, and suggesting what might be done better. Please take a moment to post a brief review of this book on his Amazon pages.

Please visit the author's website at:

www.sanmiguelallendebooks.com

www.ingramcontent.com/pod-product-compliance
Lightning Source LLC
Chambersburg PA
CBHW030938260626
47169CB00002B/523